"What type of arrangement would you like?"

Brooke waited for Matt's answer, pencil poised over her order pad. He'd been ordering flowers every day for the past two weeks, letting her know that the orders were nothing but an excuse to talk to her. He refused to deal with anyone else in the shop.

"I thought I'd send something suitable for the weather. Fresh and springlike. And these are for a very special woman, so spare no expense. I want her to know for certain that I'm interested in her."

Brooke swallowed hard, trying to ignore the sick feeling that she assured herself was *not* jealousy. "What would you like on the card?" She steeled herself for the answer.

The line was silent for a moment; then he replied in a low, husky voice. "'Gorgeous spring mornings and fragrant fresh flowers make me think of you. Anything beautiful reminds me of you.' Sign it, 'Yours anytime you want me, Matt.' Got that?"

"Yes, I have it." Brooke's hand shook as she wrote. "Where do we deliver these?"

His tone was intimate, and Brooke held her breath. "What's your home address?"

Gina Wilkins's talent and creativity are a constant source of excitement for Temptation editors. Never at a loss for a new angle, she has written five polished, satisfying Temptations, to the delight of her many readers. In *A Bright Idea* Gina has managed to find a fresh approach to the "marriage of convenience" theme, with fabulous results. And as a special treat for readers who have been eagerly awaiting the return of characters from *Cause for Celebration* (Temptation #212), Gina tells the story of Matthew and Melinda.

Gina lives with her husband and their two children in Jacksonville, Arkansas.

Books by Gina Wilkins

HARLEQUIN TEMPTATION

A Bright Idea

GINA WILKINS

Harlequin Books

TORONTO • NEW YORK • LONDON
AMSTERDAM • PARIS • SYDNEY • HAMBURG
STOCKHOLM • ATHENS • TOKYO • MILAN

For my Nashville family:
Aunt Fritzi, Uncle Shag,
Aunt Louise and Uncle Henry.

And special thanks to Joyce Chapman
of the Excelsior Hotel in Little Rock,
and to Virginia and Chris
of Double-R Florist in Jacksonville.
Thanks for all your patience!

Published April 1989

ISBN 0-373-25345-1

1

"*MARRIED!* Brooke, we're not even sleeping together!" His exasperation and amusement at his luncheon companion's proposal made Gary Wagner raise his voice a bit more than necessary, causing several heads at nearby tables to turn their way with interest. One fellow diner and inadvertent eavesdropper sitting directly behind Gary's date grinned in a manner that suggested Gary's reaction wasn't surprising. After all, the man had just been told that he was excellent husband-and-father material and then asked quite matter-of-factly if he would like to get married.

Brooke Matheny squirmed uncomfortably—not at the attention turned their way, but at Gary's response. "What's *that* got to do with anything?"

"Honey, we've been dating for four months and we've known each other for six. We're together every chance we get. Don't you think things might have progressed beyond the good-night-kiss-at-the-door stage if we were ready to discuss marriage?"

She pushed her half-empty salad plate away and twisted a bread stick between suddenly unsteady fingers. "It's just that I haven't wanted to mess up a perfectly nice relationship with sex," she explained rather obscurely. How was she supposed to explain to Gary what *she* didn't even understand herself? she wondered. She, too, had been aware of that particular lapse between them; she simply hadn't been able to picture herself actually making love with her dear friend, Gary. They'd had such a nice, close, unthreatening relationship.

He chuckled. "And exactly how did you plan to have those children you were just discussing without it?"

She glared at him. "Well, I know things would be different once we were married!" she protested. "I'm sure we'd get along just fine. You *would* want to make love to me if we were married, wouldn't you, Gary? I don't turn you off or anything, do I?" She crossed her fingers beneath the table, hoping that if they married, Brooke would be able to convince both of them that she wanted a real marriage, in every sense of the word.

His lashes closed briefly in a wince at her bluntness, then lifted again to note the dark-haired man listening with undisguised amusement from his seat behind Brooke. Frowning a bit to discourage the fellow's unwelcome attention, Gary pointedly turned his gaze back to Brooke, looking at her for a long, silent moment as he framed his answer to her anxious question.

Brooke knew Gary had long since memorized every detail of her determinedly wholesome face with its rounded cheeks, unremarkable nose, too-small mouth and too-large brown eyes. Her thick cloud of wheat-colored hair was her best feature, but even that insisted on curling in a youthful tangle around her face. No amount of makeup or effort could make Brooke look worldly or sophisticated—and she had tried for years before finally resigning herself to failure. Despite having recently passed her twenty-sixth birthday, she still occasionally had to show identification to buy a drink. Maybe Gary preferred a more obviously sensual woman, more curvaceous and experienced. Maybe that was why he hadn't pressed her for more than the casual kisses they'd exchanged during the past few months, rather than, as she'd always believed, that he'd been respecting her wishes to wait until she was absolutely sure she wanted a more intimate relationship with him.

"You don't turn me off, Brooke," Gary told her gently, as if sensing her sudden vulnerability. "In fact, I'd have made love to you a long time ago if you'd shown the slightest interest in having me do so. Face it, honey. We just don't love each other enough to marry."

"But I do love you, Gary. You know I do."

"Yes, I know." His smile held such tenderness that it brought a lump to her throat. "And I love you. But we're not *in* love."

"Oh, that."

"Yes, that," he repeated with a half grin. He placed his fork across his plate, which had once held a generous portion of spaghetti. "Some people happen to think being in love is a prerequisite for marriage, you know."

Brooke propped her elbows on the linen-covered tabletop and cupped her chin in her hands. "I hate being in love."

Gary laughed. "You sound like you've had a lot of experience with the condition."

"Enough to know I hate it. Being in love makes people stupid."

Still laughing, Gary shook his head. "Want to explain that one?"

Brooke grimaced. "People do stupid things when they're in love. They make fools of themselves. Forget all about their goals and priorities."

"That's about the most cynical thing I've ever heard you say, Brooke Matheny. Whatever happened to you to cause you to feel that way?"

She shook her head. "Never mind that. I simply decided a long time ago that when I marry, it will be for logical and practical reasons. Someone with common goals and interests, someone with a fulfilling career of his own who won't expect me to take time away from my career to cater to him, someone who'll accept that I am responsible for my own life and that I make my own decisions, both businesswise and personally. My husband and I will be equal partners in the marriage, making joint decisions while retaining autonomy. Our children will be raised with affection and support, encouraged to be anything they want to be. It's all very sensible, without the risks of an alliance based on emotions."

"And rather cold. You make it sound like a business merger, two moderately successful corporations joining forces to form a bigger, stronger institution."

"Exactly!" Brooke exclaimed triumphantly, pleased that he seemed to understand what she had in mind. "A friendly merger, of course, based on affection as well as practicality."

Gary laughed softly and shook his head. "I always knew you tried hard to be the pragmatic, sensible type, but I had no idea you carried it to this extreme. I don't think I want someone marrying me because I have nice genes to pass along to a couple of kids and because I'm so busy with my own career that I won't have time to interfere with my wife's life. I seem to be more of a romantic than I suspected. You and I have a very special friendship, Brooke Matheny. Given time and a bit of effort, it might develop into more. But unless it does, I don't want to even talk about getting married, okay?"

"*You* were the one who brought the subject up first," she reminded him. "You told me over a month ago, on your thirty-first birthday, that you've been thinking it's time you married. You said you've started to envy your friends who have wives and children and homes in the suburbs, and that, because it would be important to you, you think you could make a marriage work even though medicine is such a demanding profession."

"Brooke, I was making conversation, not proposing." He smiled, his hazel eyes affectionate beneath a boyishly unruly thatch of dark red hair. Most women took one look at that recalcitrant forelock and itched to brush it back. Brooke had occasionally given in to that impulse herself during the past four months. But now she was concentrating more on their rather unusual conversation as he continued gently. "I don't think marriage is a good idea for us."

She sighed, a bit sadly, and conceded defeat. "Okay. I guess you're right, though it seemed like a bright idea at the time. If you want a passionate, head-over-heels relationship, you deserve to have it. I just hope you don't get hurt when it happens."

He reached across the table to take her hand, leaning forward to lift it to his lips. "We both deserve to have it. No matter what you try to tell yourself, you're much too warm and loving a woman to settle for a bland, comfortable marriage. You're going to fall deeply in love someday, though it may not be with me, and when you do, you'll realize that you'd never be satisfied with less."

"No," she argued stubbornly. "You're wrong. I'm not—" She stopped speaking when Gary's electronic pager interrupted with an imperious series of beeps.

Gary glanced at the numerical readout on the face of the small plastic box. He and his staff had worked out codes so he didn't have to waste time calling in if it wasn't necessary. "Sorry, Brooke, it's an emergency. I'm going to have to leave you here."

"No problem. I've got to be going, anyway. Seems like all the men in Nashville are sending flowers to their lady friends this week. Not that I'm complaining, of course. I can take a cab back to my shop."

"The joys of dating a doctor." Gary stood and dropped a quick kiss on her cheek as he threw some bills on the table. "You may as well finish your coffee before you leave. I'll call you tonight, all right?"

Brooke nodded and watched him walk away, too wrapped up in her thoughts to notice the last repressive frown Gary turned on the dark-haired eavesdropper behind her. Sipping her coffee, she came to the decision that there would never be more than friendship between her and Gary. Forcing herself to be scrupulously honest, she admitted she'd known that for some time but just hadn't wanted to acknowledge it. He was a wonderful person and he'd make a great husband and father—but not for her or the children she longed to have. She sighed and tried to tell herself that she had plenty of time to find a compatible male who wanted the same things out of a relationship that she did. Too bad about Gary; she'd decided the life of a doctor's wife would be perfect for her. Rather than complaining about her husband's many long hours at work, she'd be perfectly content to be left to her own devices so frequently, particularly if she had children to raise.

Oh, well, she thought in resignation. She was a successful businesswoman with a rewarding and fulfilling life, and she was perfectly capable of channeling her occasional twinges of maternal instincts into more convenient pursuits.

Perhaps she'd buy a puppy, she thought wistfully.

"He's right, you know."

Brooke blinked and turned her head to find herself looking directly into a pair of beautiful, probing green eyes. Eyes that belonged to a dashing, dark-haired man in an expensive gray suit who was sitting at a tiny table just behind her, smiling at her in a manner that made her lungs go into a little spasm of excitement. Mentally telegraphing a stern order to those impertinent organs to stick to the business of breathing, she directed a cool look of inquiry toward the blatantly gorgeous male. "I beg your pardon?"

"Your friend Gary was right to turn down your marriage proposal. No man likes to think he's being pursued just because he's safe and comfortable."

Her jaw dropping at the man's unmitigated nerve, Brooke stared at him for a moment before snapping her mouth shut and setting her coffee cup firmly on the table. Turning a dismissive shoulder on the rude stranger, she reached for her purse, intending to leave without another word.

The man was beside her as she stepped into the restaurant's elegantly furnished lobby. "What? No argument?"

"I," Brooke uttered loftily, "never argue with pushy strangers. Excuse me." She moved to step around him, only to find her way blocked by his tall, athletically slender form. She glared at him in seething annoyance, trying to tell herself that she was not in the least intrigued by his tanned, classically handsome face, nor close to being mesmerized by his thick-lashed, just slightly uptilted eyes as they smiled down into hers. She was lying to herself, of course.

"You have a very interesting philosophy on falling in love," the man continued, undaunted by her furious expression. "I'd like to hear more. Maybe I could buy you a drink or dinner sometime?"

Suddenly finding herself fighting a ridiculous urge to laugh at the man's total lack of scruples in admitting that he'd listened in on an obviously personal conversation, Brooke managed somehow to keep her expression impassive. "Look, if you were eavesdropping on everything my friend and I were saying, you should have gotten the idea that I'm not in the market for an affair. If I'm looking for anything, it's marriage and children. Find yourself another woman to pick up in a restaurant."

He laughed, a quick, rich sound of amusement that sent her lungs *and* her heart into some kind of weird mating dance. Brooke decided to get out of this guy's company and then have a long, stern talk with her internal organs.

"Maybe I'm not quite desperate enough for feminine companionship to resort to picking up beautiful young women in restaurants," the man suggested when he'd stopped laughing. "Maybe I'm interested in the same things you are."

Beautiful? Ridiculous. He *was* giving her a line. But it was a rather nice line, Brooke thought fleetingly. "Happy hunting," she told him, stepping around him.

He made no effort to stop her, but followed her outside into the crisp March afternoon. "What's the matter, Brooke? Think I might be the guy who'd make you do something stupid?" he challenged her.

She really should have just walked on. Instead she stopped, looked into those bottomless green eyes of his and sighed deeply. "I don't just think it. I know it," she muttered glumly.

Surprise and something else crossed his face, but she didn't take time to stop and analyze it. She turned and walked away, as fast as she could without actually running. She was in a cab and on her way toward her florist shop before she allowed herself to relax in relief.

Funny, she actually felt as if she'd just escaped a very dangerous situation. She also felt a bit like a coward.

"No. ABSOLUTELY NOT!" Matt's raised voice reverberated through his sedately furnished office, causing his secretary to wince at her desk on the other side of a partially open door. She'd heard *that* tone before, and it always meant the boss was about to lay down the law. She glanced at the prim young woman sitting in a low leather chair, waiting to keep an appointment with Mr. James and trying hard to pretend she couldn't hear every clearly spoken word from the other room.

The pretty strawberry blonde facing Matt across his desk didn't even flinch at the words she'd heard many, many times. "I'm going to Europe for the summer," she repeated firmly. "With Parker Hadley. Backpacking. Whether you loan me the money I need or not."

"Over my dead body."

"If that's the way you want it," his sister answered equably.

"If you really think I'm going to allow you to go off to Europe for the summer with some guy you only met a few weeks ago, you've lost your mind." Matt leaned his full weight on his doubled fists, which rested on his desk, and faced his younger sister with deadly determination. "Remember, Melinda, I met this guy when I was home on vacation last week. He's got all the character of a tree frog. He's also well aware that your two older sisters are married to wealthy businessmen, and he probably thinks you've got a bit of money yourself."

"How dare you judge my friends on the basis of one meeting?" Melinda asked furiously. "You think just because you supervise God only knows how many people in this oversize, overpriced hotel you're an expert judge of character, I suppose. Let me remind you you've never been all that great at judging the people I know! You've thought half my boyfriends were criminals, and you were wrong about all of them!"

"Look, I've learned a lot about people in the past five years," Matt returned, trying to speak calmly and rationally to the nineteen-year-old sister who could always make him lose his temper faster than anyone else he knew. "I've dealt with good, hardworking people and with scum. Thieves, opportunists, pimps, the kind of lowlife that expensive convention locations such as this one attract. I can spot a guy who's out for a fast buck, hoping for a free ride. That joker you're planning to go off to Europe with is one of them! And this time I'm not mistaken!"

Melinda let out a furious breath and whirled away from him, crossing her arms stubbornly over her chest. "I won't listen to you! I should have known better than to come to you for your support."

"You should have known that if Merry opposed your idea, *I* certainly wouldn't go along with it," he agreed coolly, naming the older sister who'd been Melinda's guardian since their parents had died ten years earlier. "Hadley's not fit to be responsible for you in Europe. Lord, haven't you read the newspapers lately? There are terrorists everywhere, bombs going off, kidnappings. If you're that set on going, let me arrange a safe European tour for you with chaperons and guides. Meaghan could go, too," he added, referring to her more level-headed twin sister.

"To keep an eye on me, right?" Melinda inquired scornfully. "Well, forget it. I don't need a chaperon. And Parker wouldn't have to be responsible for me. I'd be responsible for myself."

"Oh, boy, is *that* comforting!" Matt was unable to resist that bit of sarcasm, though he knew full well it wouldn't accomplish anything but to make his sister angrier.

He was right. Melinda slammed her flattened palms down on his desk, facing him in much the same pose he was in, chin up, shoulders squared, mouth set in resolution. "Dammit, Matt, I'm almost twenty. And I'm bored! I'm tired of going to school, tired of studying and doing what everyone wants. I need to do something different, something adventurous, or I'm going to go nuts! Why can't anyone understand that?"

"I thought you wanted to be a psychologist. Whatever happened to all those lofty ideals you used to spout about helping people work out their problems?"

"How can I help other people with their lives when I've never even lived a life of my own?" Melinda demanded.

"So you're planning on sleeping with this Hadley guy across Europe, risking life and limb for no other reason than being bored? That's a fine, mature bit of rationalization, Melinda," he told her grimly.

He was rather surprised when Melinda flushed deeply. "I'm *not* sleeping with Parker! But even if I were, it would be no one's business but mine."

Matt drew a deep breath, lifting a hand to rub a suddenly throbbing temple. Hell, he thought in disgust, he dealt with one crisis after another every day in his job as manager of the majestic Amber Rose Hotel in Nashville. Why couldn't he handle one impulsive, foolish young sister? And why was he suddenly feeling sorry for her as he looked into her unhappy green eyes? He tried to remember being nineteen and restless—only eleven years earlier, actually. It would have been the last year his parents were alive, his second year in college. Come to think of it, that was the year he'd worried his folks so by taking up motorcycle racing. Because he'd been bored and thought himself in need of adventure.

"Melinda," he said more quietly, trying to reach through her stubborn resolution. "I have an appointment that I have to take care of. But I want you to know that I've listened to what you've said, and I understand, a little, how you feel. We'll talk more later, okay? In the meantime, why don't you go down to the dress shop and charge yourself a new dress in my name? You can wear it tonight when I take you out to dinner."

"It won't work, Matt," she told him suspiciously. "You're not going to buy me off."

He made a real effort to hold on to his temper. "I'm not trying to buy you off. I just want to talk to you later when we have more time, all right? I'll see you in the suite in a couple of hours."

Melinda rolled her eyes but seemed to accept her dismissal. "You can talk all you want, but *I'm* the one who's going to make the decisions for my life," she warned over her shoulder as she made her exit, determined to have the last word. "You just remember that, Matthew James!"

Matt moaned and dropped his chin, closing his eyes for a moment. Lord, he thought ruefully, he'd rather handle an embezzling desk clerk any day than to try to get through to Melinda. Why in the world had she gotten on a bus in Missouri, where she lived with their sister and her husband, and come to him in Nashville? Melinda and Matt had *never* gotten along that well! It had been suggested that it was because they were entirely too much alike.

Remembering the appointment his secretary had warily announced sometime earlier, Matt sighed and straightened, reaching out to his telephone. He pushed a button. "You can send her in now, Carol."

Just what he needed, he thought wearily. Some florist was going to make a pitch to him about what she could do for the Amber Rose as a steady customer. He'd tried to palm her off on the purchasing department, but the woman had been stubbornly persistent, insisting on talking directly to the manager. Ah, well, he was an expert on dealing with pushy salespeople. Hell, he added silently with a grin, he'd just survived an encounter with Melinda, hadn't he?

He looked up without much enthusiasm when someone entered his office, then narrowed his eyes in surprise when his gaze fell on the attractive young woman who faced him in equal astonishment. It had been two weeks since he'd overheard the prosaic proposal of marriage at the luncheon table next to his, but he hadn't forgotten it, nor the lovely woman who'd made the outrageous suggestion to her flustered companion. For some reason he hadn't quite been able to get her out of his mind, though he'd thought at the time that the woman was badly in need of being taken down a peg. Too cocky for his tastes, too coldly practical. He'd enjoyed rattling her by mocking her overheard conversation. Oddly enough, he'd even been a bit disappointed when she'd flatly turned down his invitation for a drink.

Now he found himself staring at that same young woman across his desk, facing him from the very same spot his defiant sister had occupied moments before. He looked into the huge brown eyes that, widened with surprise as they were now, seemed to take up half her face. And he felt as if someone had kicked his knees out from under him. He put a hand on his desk in a casual pose designed to hide the fact that he was holding himself upright. "Well, hello...Brooke, wasn't it?" he commented with what sounded even to him like cool amusement. "Did you decide to take me up on that offer for a drink? Or are you here to check out *my* genes?"

2

BROOKE DREW IN a quick breath on a surge of sheer fury, turned on one heel and started out of the office. Forget the account, she told herself seethingly. It was bad enough that this guy had made fun of her two weeks ago, immediately after listening in on her private conversation. But to remind her of it now in such a mocking manner was unforgivable.

"Hey, wait a minute!" The dark-haired man with the memorable green eyes—she knew now his name was Matthew James—spoke quickly and with a startled laugh as he hurried around his desk to stop her from leaving. "Where are you going?"

"Out," she returned flatly.

He stepped in front of her, barring her path. He moved fast, she had to give him that, she thought grudgingly. But then he looked like the type who'd have lots of fast moves. None of which could catch her. "Please let me go," she requested coolly.

"Look, I'm sorry about what I said, okay?" He had just the right touch of regret in his tone. "I was surprised at seeing you again and I made a bad joke."

She kept her expression impassive, determined not to be swayed by the rueful smile that had suddenly appeared on the face that just wouldn't leave her mind during the past two weeks. "That seems to be a habit of yours, Mr. James," she informed him.

He winced, then smiled again. "Yes, I'll admit it is. Now will you forgive me and let us get on with whatever brought you here, Brooke—er, Miss . . . ?"

"Matheny." She supplied her name reluctantly, her chin lowering a bit. She was *not* staying because of his apology, she told herself clearly. Nor was she staying because of the faintest glimmer of remorse in his eyes at her discomfiture. She was staying only because he happened to manage a hotel that would be a profitable client for her florist shop, Ribbons & Blossoms. She took a quick, deep breath and extended her hand, her voice coolly professional when she spoke again. "I own Ribbons & Blossoms, Mr. James, and I'd like to talk to you about doing business with the Amber Rose. I believe I can offer you excellent results at much better prices than you are currently paying for floral service."

Lingering over the handshake just a bit longer than was necessary, Matt finally released her and waved her to the chair beside his desk. "Please have a seat," he urged her, taking his own massive leather desk chair and leaning back to regard her over steepled fingers. His position emphasized the leanly muscular form beneath his beautifully tailored gray suit. Brooke kept her eyes trained on his face. "Tell me, Miss Matheny, why did you refuse to talk to our purchasing department about your services? As I'm sure you were informed, all buying is done by that department. I don't handle this sort of thing personally."

Brooke folded her hands neatly in her lap—trying to ignore that the one he'd pressed in his was still tingling like crazy—and told herself to be grateful that he'd suddenly become all business. Even if his tone wasn't particularly encouraging. She hoped her face didn't reveal her sudden embarrassment as she remembered the last words they'd spoken to each other two weeks earlier.

"What's the matter, Brooke? Think I might be the guy who'd make you do something stupid?"

"I don't just think it. I know it."

Whatever had made her say *that*?

"I attempted to talk to Mr. Quelling, the manager of your purchasing department, several times, Mr. James. I could never even get past the door. And then I discovered that the florist currently servicing your hotel is owned in part by Mr. Quelling's brother. Perhaps you already know that...." She paused delicately.

Matt only looked at her, revealing nothing. "Go on."

"Anyway, I wouldn't have made such a pest of myself, but I'm a loyal patron of this hotel, Mr. James. I dine in your restaurant quite often and I enjoy the performers you book for your lounge. That's why it disturbs me, both as a customer and a florist, to see that your first-rate hotel is getting second-rate service and probably paying high prices."

Matt frowned. "What do you mean by second-rate service?"

"I dropped by this morning for a glance at the tables where your guests were having breakfast. Are you aware that their tables were decorated with two daisies and a bit of greenery in white milk-glass bud vases?" she demanded, unable to keep genuine indignation from coloring the professional tone she was trying to maintain. "Daisies! Any little diner can furnish daisies on the breakfast table, Mr. James. But the Amber Rose should provide something more lovely, more exotic to greet your guests as they begin their busy days. For what you're probably paying for those daisies, I can provide you with Star of Bethlehem, or freesia, perhaps. Freesia have such a lovely fragrance to wake up to."

Realizing she'd digressed into a discussion of her favorite subject—flowers—and away from the more practical topic under discussion, she quickly went on to outline the other services Ribbons & Blossoms could provide. Matt listened impassively until she finished, his intensely perceptive eyes never leaving her face. When she fell silent, waiting for a response—*any* response—he straightened in his chair and leaned slightly forward. "You have a business card, Miss Matheny?"

"Yes, of course." That wasn't exactly what she'd hoped for, but it was better than nothing. She quickly extracted one of her cleverly designed floral decorated business cards from her small clutch bag and extended it to him. "Do you have any questions I could answer for you at this time, Mr. James?"

"Not at this time," he returned gravely, making her wonder if he were mocking her carefully polite manner. But he didn't smile as he added, "I'll pass your card along to our purchasing department. Someone will be in touch with you, I assure you."

She'd struck out. Brooke stifled a sigh, telling herself she shouldn't be surprised. She'd hardly given him a first impression of a levelheaded, competent business-woman. He was probably convinced she was an idiot. She squared her shoulders and stood, automatically straightening the skirt of the crisp winter-white suit she wore with a turquoise silk blouse. At least she *looked* professional, she thought with little satisfaction. "Thank you for taking the time to see me, Mr. James."

"You think maybe you could call me Matt now that our business meeting is over?" he asked unexpectedly, walking around the desk to stand close to her. Too close to her, she decided as her rate of respiration increased sharply.

She took a small step backward, trying to appear nonchalant. She didn't really see the need to call him *anything* now that their business meeting was over, but she refrained from pointing that out. Instead, she smiled faintly and repeated her thanks, inching toward the door. "Goodbye," she added, purposely leaving off any form of address.

"Surely you don't believe this is goodbye," he chided her, almost indulgently. He'd followed her, never allowing her to put more than a few inches between them.

She eyed him warily, noting in resignation that he'd once again managed to insinuate himself between her and the door. "Of course I'd be happy to answer any questions you have about my *business* in the future," she told him.

"I'm not a big believer in fate," Matt surprised her by saying almost conversationally, "but there has to be a reason we keep running into each other. Have dinner with me tonight, Brooke, and let's find out what destiny has planned for us, shall we?"

She surprised them both with a laugh. "Well, it's a great line," she admitted, "but I'm afraid I'm no more a believer in fate than you are, Mr. James." She pronounced the formal version of his name quite clearly. "We've run into each other because we both happened to lunch at the same restaurant two weeks ago and because I'd love to have your hotel as a client.

"Not that I knew the manager was the same man I'd met once before," she added hastily. "I was as surprised as you were when I walked in here to find you. As far as destiny goes, I hope the future holds a long, satisfactory business association for us, but a more personal relationship is out of the question."

His smile never faltered. "Why?"

Remember what a big account he controls, Brooke warned her volatile temper. "Because I'm not interested, Mr. James," she heard herself saying. There may have been a more diplomatic response, but something told her diplomacy wouldn't go very far with this persistent male.

He stepped aside with a tauntingly polite little gesture. "I'll be seeing you, Brooke. And maybe next time we'll test the truth of that declaration."

She could either stalk away in chill dignity, leaving him with the last word, or hit him. She prudently chose the former option.

Matt watched her swiftly cross his secretary's office and let herself out the door into the hallway, never once looking over her shoulder, though he suspected she knew he was watching. Only when she'd disappeared from his sight did he toss a quick look at his deferential secretary. "Please get Alan Quelling from purchasing on the phone, Carol. Tell him I want to see him. Now."

He toyed with Brooke's card as he waited for Quelling. The card reminded him of her, he thought with a slight smile, his gaze lingering on the stylized tulips and ribbons bordering the creamy yellow rectangle. Unique, pretty and quite practical. Having met her again, he found himself more intrigued than ever. And he intended to see her again, in more promising circumstances. He thought briefly of her proposal to that other man, then dismissed it. She wasn't in love with that other guy. She'd been acting on impulse, he was quite sure. It would do her good to put such silly ideas behind her and concentrate on a man who was more than "comfortable." A man such as himself.

His smile faded when he looked up to find Alan Quelling from purchasing standing nervously in his doorway. "Come in, Quelling. I want to talk about our florist account."

Quelling paled but stepped bravely into his employer's office.

BROOKE HAD NOT CALMED DOWN by the time the glass elevator deposited her in the luxurious lobby of the Amber Rose. She was reluctant to go back to her shop with her cheeks flaming with wrath, her eyes doubtlessly glittering with fury. Her anger mounted even more, if possible, at Matthew James for getting beneath her skin this way, putting a crack in her carefully cultivated professional veneer. Her gaze paused on the tasteful stained-glass sign across the crowded lobby that designated the bar. Maybe a soft drink and a few minutes to herself would help her regain her control.

She slipped into a tiny booth and ordered a diet cola with a twist of lemon. While she waited for the beverage to arrive, she was finally forced to admit that she was as angry with herself as she was with Matt—well, almost. What was it about him that attracted her, made her so intensely aware of him even as he infuriated her? She knew what she *didn't* like about him. He was a bossy, overbearing male. If she hadn't known already from his pushy remarks the first time she'd laid eyes on him, she would have learned from the overheard conversation with his sister. Obviously he was a man who considered his word law, who'd allowed an impressive, highly responsible position to inflate his concept of his own importance. A long way from the comfortable, easily managed type of man she'd dated in the past few years. Matt James was exactly the type of man she *didn't* want to get involved with.

So what was it about him that turned her into jelly when he stood too close? That made the image of his face linger in her memory even after that brief, uncomfortable meeting two weeks ago? That tempted her to accept his offers to buy her dinner even as she saw red over the manner in which he asked?

"Driven you to drink, has he?"

The dry question drew Brooke's startled gaze upward to the colorfully clad, attractive young blonde who'd paused by the booth to speak to her. Recognizing Matt's sister, Brooke hesitated, then asked carefully, "I beg your pardon?"

"You went in to see my brother after he and I finished yelling at each other, and now you're in the bar," Melinda clarified blithely. "I'm not at all surprised. He affects me that way, too."

Brooke had to laugh. "Actually I'm having a diet soda," she explained. The waitress appeared just then to set the drink in question on the table. Brooke paused only momentarily before asking Melinda if she'd like to join her.

Melinda didn't hesitate even that long. She promptly slid into the other side of the booth. "I'll have the same thing she's having," she informed the waitress, then smiled brightly across the table. "Hi. I'm Melinda James—Matt's sister."

"I figured that out," Brooke returned wryly. Even if she hadn't overheard the conversation, Brooke would have known Melinda was related to Matt. Though Melinda's thick, shoulder-length waves were an unusual strawberry blond while Matt's neatly cropped hair was a rich brown, the siblings had both been blessed with deep green eyes, fringed in luxurious dark lashes and slightly uptilted at the corners. Though Melinda was delicately pretty, unquestionably feminine, and Matt the epitome of virile masculinity, their facial resemblance was evident. "My name's Brooke Matheny."

"Are you a friend of Matt's?"

Brooke shook her head. "No, actually, I'm a local florist trying to obtain the Amber Rose as an account. Your brother and I only met—formally—today."

"Formally?" Melinda repeated, tilting her head.

Wondering what had possessed her to say it quite that way, Brooke nodded. "We, uh, sort of ran into each other a couple of weeks ago when we both had lunch at the same restaurant."

Seeming to be satisfied with that explanation, Melinda propped her elbows on the table and rested her chin on her linked hands. "So, did you get the account?"

With a little grimace Brooke shrugged. "I doubt it."

"How come?" Melinda clearly believed in plain speaking and satisfying an obviously healthy curiosity in the most direct manner possible.

"I don't think I made too great an impression."

Pursing her skillfully painted lips, Melinda gave Brooke a thorough inspection. "I find that hard to believe," she said at last. "Didn't he ask you out or anything? I would've given Matt more credit than that."

Brooke's eyes widened. "What do you mean."

"Well, you're great looking and really nice. You seem to be just the type of woman Matt would be interested in. Unless you're married or something?"

Brooke laughed, liking Melinda James despite herself. She found the unusual conversation rather like dealing with an endearingly precocious child, though Melinda was hardly a child. Simply a stunning young woman who refused to play verbal games. "No, I'm not married or something."

"So, did he ask you out?"

"As a matter of fact, he did," Brooke answered in good-natured resignation. "And I turned him down because he made me furious. I found him rather arrogant, entirely too self-assured and decidedly autocratic."

"Yeah, that's Matt," Melinda agreed gaily, accepting her soft drink from the waitress. "He's also gorgeous, isn't he?"

"Uh—"

"I know sisters aren't supposed to notice things like that, but, hey, I've got eyes. He's a good-looking devil, even if it *is* a wonder that he's made it to age thirty without someone strangling him."

"Thirty?" Brooke was startled. She hadn't realized Matt was so young. He had the self-possession of a man several years older, as well as a position of authority that would normally be granted only after years of experience. The Amber Rose was one of the top three hotels in the Nashville area, which was saying a lot in Tennessee's Music City, the center of the country music industry. Now that she thought about it, she supposed she *had* noticed that he looked young, but she'd just assumed he was in the latter half of his thirties. "He's done quite well for himself to be so young."

Melinda nodded glumly. "I just hate it when he gets a promotion. Always goes straight to his head." She sipped her cola, then chuckled. "Gosh, I sound like I can't stand him. The truth is, I'm nuts about him. I'd like to boil him in oil most of the time, of course, but he's really a sweetie when you get to know him."

A sweetie? Brooke could think of several adjectives for Matthew James, but "sweetie" wasn't one of them. "Um—"

"Yeah. I plan to work for him this summer. Think we'll survive?"

Thoroughly confused, Brooke frowned. "You plan to work for him this summer. But I thought—" She faltered, then shrugged and went on. "I couldn't help overhearing part of your discussion with your brother earlier. I thought you wanted to backpack across Europe for the summer."

Melinda laughed. "That's what I want everyone to think," she confided, leaning forward across the small table. "Actually I want to work here in the Amber Rose. Working for Merry's fun—that's my older sister; she owns a theme-party service in Missouri—but I've been doing it for ages and I want to try something different. I'm on spring break now from Southwest Missouri State University, and I decided it was as good a time as any to set up my plans for the summer."

"But why didn't you just ask your brother for a job?"

"Oh, then he'd give me something really boring. You know, like cleaning rooms. He doesn't believe in special favors for family, you understand. This way if he thinks he has to bribe me to keep me from doing something stupid, he'll offer something more interesting, hoping to entice me. But don't tell him, okay?"

Brooke shook her head in a mixture of dismay and admiration. "Melinda James, you are a very dangerous young woman."

Melinda gave a comical effort to look innocent. "Gee, that's what Merry, Marsha and Meaghan always say."

"Who?"

"My sisters. Merry's the oldest, then Marsha. Meaghan's my twin."

"Twin? Oh, my God, there are *two* of you?" Brooke asked with an exaggerated gasp.

Laughing in delight, Melinda patted Brooke's hand. "I like you, you know? I really do."

"I like you, too," Brooke replied, being absolutely truthful. She thought Matthew James's little sister was delightful.

"You know, I think you'd be good for Matt. I wish you'd reconsider going out with him."

Brooke's smile faded abruptly. She looked quickly at her watch. "Oops. I'd better get back to my shop."

Melinda frowned her dissatisfaction with the obvious ruse but made no effort to detain her new friend. "Maybe I'll look you up when I'm in Nashville this summer. We could catch a movie or something together."

"I'd like that," Brooke replied sincerely. "Call me at my shop. Ribbons & Blossoms."

"Cute name. See you, Brooke." ˙

"See you, Melinda." She was quite sure she *would* see the younger woman. Brooke had no doubt that if Melinda James had set her mind to working at the Amber Rose for the summer, she would do just that. She rather looked forward to seeing Melinda again, though she felt as if she'd just stepped off a carnival ride—a little dizzy. She just hoped Melinda managed to resist her obvious desire to do a bit of matchmaking between Matt and Brooke. Brooke had her work cut out for her just to resist her own inexplicable temptation to spend more time with Matthew James.

BROOKE PLACED the last yellow rose in the tall crystal vase just as Rhonda, one of her employees, called her to the telephone. "Just a sec," she called back, tagging the expensive arrangement and sliding it into one of the huge refrigerated units to wait for delivery. Some wife was going to be delighted on her anniversary, she thought with satisfaction as she took one last look at the lovely blooms. And then she headed for the telephone.

"Brooke Matheny."

"Hello, Brooke Matheny."

It wasn't necessary for him to identify himself, though it had been a full week since she'd last heard his voice. Brooke's fingers tightened convulsively around the telephone receiver. "Hello, Mr. James."

The exasperated sigh came through the line quite clearly. "Matt. The name is Matt. Can you say Matt?" he added in an imitation of Mr. Rogers.

She couldn't help smiling, but at least he didn't know that. "All right. Matt," she conceded.

"Very good," he approved. "Now ask me why I called."

"Why did you call?" she parroted obediently.

"To ask you to lunch. Now say, thank you, Matt, I'd—"

"I'm sorry, Matt, but I'm really quite busy today," she broke in firmly. Obviously he hadn't believed her when she'd told him she wasn't interested in going out with him. Well, she could be just as stubborn as he.

"Too busy for a business lunch to discuss a lucrative new account?" he asked in exaggerated surprise.

"You really just want to discuss business?" she asked suspiciously, not believing it for a minute.

"If you're not interested in doing business with the Amber Rose . . ." He left the sentence hanging suggestively.

Damn him. Extortion. Not that she'd ever thought he'd be above such methods. He wasn't even making an effort to conceal it, but sounded amused, as if *he* knew that *she* knew exactly what he was doing. "I'm interested in the account."

"Then what do you say we meet at Smitty's at twelve-thirty? We can talk more about it then."

"All right. But it's only to discuss your account," she added firmly, then sighed when she found herself talking to a dial tone. "The man should definitely be strangled," she muttered, reminded of Melinda's words as she hung up.

"Sounds interesting. What man?"

Brooke looked up to find Rhonda leaning against a counter in the momentary break from customers and smiling impudently at her employer, her plump face creased with the grin. "That was Matthew James," she replied. "Manager of the Amber Rose. He wants to meet me for lunch to discuss possibly doing business with us."

"Sounds encouraging. I thought you said we weren't going to get that one."

"I'm beginning to wonder if it's worth it."

Rhonda arched an eyebrow in interest. "Maybe you should tell me more about this guy."

Reprieve came in the form of a sudden rush of customers. Brooke inhaled gratefully and pasted on her work smile. She just wasn't up to talking about Matthew James. Not now, anyway. She was too busy trying to keep herself from hyperventilating at the thought of having lunch with him. Damn him.

3

A PLACE BROOKE HAD always considered a "yuppie hamburger joint," Smitty's was loud and crowded and eclectically decorated. The establishment also happened to offer the best burgers in Nashville. Brooke was already anticipating a cheese-and-bacon Smitty Burger as she pushed open the heavy leaded-glass and oak door. Despite the crowd, her eyes focused immediately on one dark-suited, dark-haired male standing at the reception desk flirting outrageously with the miniskirted receptionist. Brooke found herself scowling as the statuesque young brunette laughed at something Matt said and slapped him playfully on the arm. Then she immediately forced herself to smile. It was certainly no concern of hers if Matt James was the type of man to try to pick up one woman while waiting to have lunch with another, she told herself with a mental sniff.

As if sensing the waves of disapproval coming at him from the doorway, Matt looked up, caught her eye and smiled. And Brooke's insides melted. Fighting an urge to turn and run screaming from the restaurant, she stepped bravely into danger. "Hello, Matt."

"Brooke." He took her hand and held on to it, his eyes taking an almost intimate survey. "You look lovely."

She had to keep reminding herself that he was some sort of expert on murmuring things designed to melt the coldest willpower. She knew she looked just as she always did, though she was perversely pleased that she'd worn her favorite red shirtwaist dress, the one that emphasized her slender waist and added becoming color to her fair cheeks. "Thank you." She tugged her hand out of his.

"Ready for your table, Matt?" the receptionist inquired, her brilliant blue eyes lingering on Brooke with open curiosity.

"Yeah, thanks, Lynette."

Lynette led them to a relatively secluded little booth in one corner, her slim hips moving seductively beneath the denim miniskirt. Brooke refused to look at Matt to see if he was admiring the performance. She was sure that he was.

"See you later, Matt. Don't forget about Sunday."

"No, I won't," Matt promised with a smile, then looked at Brooke as Lynette walked away. "Have you eaten here before?"

"Many times," she replied, burying her face in a menu, though she knew exactly what she'd order. Of course she'd have to fake an appetite. For some reason, hers had disappeared.

Don't forget about Sunday. The man should definitely be strangled. The sultry Lynette wasn't a day older than the sister he seemed so determined to overprotect. Hadn't he ever heard of hypocrisy?

"Something wrong, Brooke?" Matt was watching her with that infuriating smile in his eyes, as if he knew exactly what she was thinking. She hoped he did, she told herself emphatically.

"No, Matt, nothing's wrong," she lied calmly. Closing her menu, she reached for the slender, soft leather briefcase she'd brought with her. "I brought along some figures to go over with you. Exactly what Ribbons & Blossoms can do for you and at what price."

"Why don't you save that for the new purchasing department manager?" Matt suggested smoothly, pushing his own unopened menu aside. "I gave her your card last week, and she promised she'd contact you. She's going to be talking to several florists in the next week or so. You'll be given a fair chance at the account, I assure you."

Brooke took a deep breath and counted to ten. "You mean," she said at last, her voice dangerously low, "that you invited me to lunch only to tell me that you've turned my card over to your purchasing department?"

"You're being obtuse again, Brooke," he chided her gently, still smiling. "You're much too bright to continue to insist you don't know I'm interested in more than your business. I'm interested in *you*, Brooke Matheny. I have been since I first saw you."

"You," she told him furiously, "are a—"

"Hey, Matt, how ya doin'?" a booming voice interrupted. "Lyn told me you were here again. Ain't you got no place else where you can eat lunch?"

Matt's laugh told Brooke that he knew quite well he'd just been saved a succinct, decidedly uncomplimentary summation of his character. He turned his head to grin at the man who'd approached. "Guess I'm just a glutton for punishment, Smitty. You know how much I enjoy having my stomach pumped."

The short, heavyset, nearly bald man roared with laughter and cuffed Matt none too gently on the jaw. "I oughta ban you from my place, you young smart aleck. Would, too, if I wasn't makin' so much money off you."

Brooke could barely stop herself from staring. *This* was Smitty? The owner of one of the most popular young professional hangouts in Nashville? He looked as if he could make a fortune as a character actor, playing two-bit hoods and ex-cons. His oddly pleasant-ugly face was decorated with a three-inch scar down one lined, tanned cheek, both meaty arms bore colorful tattoos beneath his rolled-up plaid shirtsleeves, his stomach pushed out beyond his belt but looked as if it would take a fist without even slowing him down. Yet his eyes were bright blue and friendly, his crooked smile appealing. And he'd just given Matt a thump that had shaken a lock down over his forehead and left him fingering his jaw with rueful caution.

Brooke smiled brilliantly at Smitty. She was going to like this guy.

Matt frowned repressively at Brooke's obvious pleasure in seeing him hit, then nodded toward Smitty. "Brooke Matheny, meet the owner of this sleazy joint, George Smith. He's also Lynette's father, though how this ugly character could produce such a lovely daughter is totally beyond me. If I didn't know for a fact that Margie Smith is the most loyal and moral woman I've ever met, I'd be looking around for a blue-eyed mailman."

This time Brooke couldn't quite stop herself from staring. Lynette's father?

"Nice to meet you, Miss Matheny," Smitty told her with what sounded like approval. "A pretty young woman like you shouldn't be so hard up for company that you'd lower yourself to have lunch with this smart-mouthed kid."

"My thoughts, exactly," Brooke agreed sweetly, making Matt choke across the table. She smiled brightly at him, genuinely amused at his expression.

Smitty nodded his approval. "I like this one, Matthew."

"So do I, Smitty." Even Matt's voice was lethal, she discovered with a hard swallow, when he lowered it to such a meaningfully intimate level. "The problem is," he continued in much the same tone, "she doesn't like me."

"Can't say's I blame her," Smitty commented thoughtfully. He winked at Brooke. "Still, you might give him a chance, ma'am. He's really okay once ya get to know him a little better."

Brooke wisely declined to comment.

"Here's your waitress. She'll take good care of ya. You haven't forgotten about Sunday, have you, Matt?"

Matt shook his head. "No, Smitty, I haven't forgotten. Tell Margie I'll be there."

Smitty nodded toward Brooke. "Feel free to bring a guest if ya want. Talk at ya later."

Brooke and Matt placed their orders without looking at each other—or at least she assumed he wasn't looking at her. She refused to check.

"Brooke," he said firmly when the waitress had left them alone. "Look at me."

She didn't waste her time arguing with him. Her eyes met his in defiance.

"Do you have any idea how beautiful you are when you smile?" he murmured, surprising her yet again.

"When are you going to smile at me the way you smiled at Smitty, lovely Brooke?"

"Don't hold your breath," she advised him.

"Are you always this belligerent?" he asked curiously.

Her shoulders slumped a bit. "No," she admitted finally. "I'm never this belligerent. Something about you just seems to bring out the worst in me."

He appeared to take encouragement from that reluctant confession. "If it makes you feel any better, I have that same effect on a lot of people. My younger sister, particularly. I don't mean to."

Choosing to let that comment pass, she concentrated instead on his reference to his sisters. "I met Melinda last week. Did she tell you?"

"Yes. She likes you very much."

"I like her, too. I enjoyed talking to her."

Matt grimaced. "I suppose she told you all about her bossy, infuriating older brother."

"She mentioned you in passing."

He chuckled. "I'll bet. I suppose she also tried to convince you that I should approve of this wild scheme of hers to backpack across Europe with that Hadley guy."

Brooke shrugged and murmured something noncommittal as her burger plate was set in front of her. She dipped a thick, skin-on fried potato strip in catsup and lifted it to her mouth.

"I'm not going to allow her to do it, you know," Matt stated, pouring catsup on his own plate.

"She's almost twenty. I don't see how you can stop her," Brooke commented.

He looked up with narrowed eyes. "I'll stop her. I love my sister, but she's got the common sense of a turnip sometimes. She has no idea what could happen to a beautiful young woman in a foreign country. She speaks no other languages, has been raised in a sheltered environment, has hardly traveled out of Missouri. I'm not going to let her put herself in that kind of danger. I've offered her a job for the summer at the Amber Rose," he added.

Brooke tried to look surprised. "Have you?"

"Yeah." He seemed quite pleased with himself. "I knew she wouldn't go for maid work, but she seemed a bit intrigued by the idea of working in the personnel office. She doesn't want me to know that she's interested, of course, so I didn't push her. I gave her a few weeks to think it over. She has to decide that it was her idea all along, you understand," he disclosed in amusement.

Brooke took a big gulp of her cola to swallow the laughter that threatened. She wouldn't betray Melinda's confidence, of course, but it was tempting to shake this man's arrogance a bit. Her amusement faded when she realized that she actually found Matt's determined protection of his little sister endearing. Which was ridiculous. Any older brother would want to protect his sister, she told herself impatiently, and would probably be more tactful about expressing his opinions. Matt seemed to think that all he should do was say no and Melinda should immediately acquiesce to him. No discussion.

Matt had a lot in common with Brooke's father.

On that depressing thought, her appetite faded again. They ate in silence for a while, and then she set her half-eaten burger back on her plate. "I'm still angry with you for misleading me about the purpose of this lunch," she informed him, taking the offensive.

"I knew you wouldn't agree to meet me if you didn't think it was business," he returned with his own form of logic.

"That's right. I told you, Matt, I don't want to go out with you. I know what you want and I'm not interested."

He pushed his well-cleaned plate away and crossed his forearms on the table. "Just what is it you think I want?"

Her cheeks warmed at his bluntness, but she was determined to be equally frank. "An affair."

"And what makes you think that?"

The blush spread. She felt like a fool. She was hardly the type of woman who had men chasing her around desks and begging for her body. But she wasn't completely stupid. She knew desire when she saw it. For some incomprehensible reason, Matt James wanted her. She saw it in his eyes even now as he watched her steadily, waiting for her answer. Her body tightened with her own wholly unwelcome answering desire. "Don't you?"

He acknowledged the soft question with a nod. "Yes. I want you, Brooke. Have from the first."

"Well, then—" she began, more shaken than ever by hearing it put into words.

"But," he interrupted firmly, "not just an affair. I'm not a man who indulges in a string of casual affairs, Brooke. I grew up with four sisters. I like women and I respect them. I don't use them.

"Lynette," he continued when her eyes flicked involuntarily toward the reception desk, "is the daughter of a friend. I've known her since she was fifteen and I regard her almost as another little sister. You really thought I was trying to make time with her while I was waiting for you to arrive, didn't you?"

"Yes," she admitted, looking down.

"Why do you have such a low opinion of me, Brooke? What is it about me that makes you want to dislike me?"

Her lashes flew up at the tone in which he'd asked the questions. If she hadn't known better, she'd have thought she'd heard vulnerability, even a bit of hurt in his voice. She found him still watching her in that disturbing, unwavering manner of his. "I don't care for overbearing men," she heard herself answering him honestly.

"You think I'm overbearing?"

"I think you're entirely too fond of having your own way. I couldn't help overhearing part of your conversation with Melinda last week. And look at the way you manipulated me to get me here. It doesn't seem to bother you in the least that you deceived me just to suit your own purposes."

His expression turned thoughtful as he considered her words. "I suppose I am used to having my own way," he concurred. "Comes from being the only boy in a family of five kids, I suppose, though I wasn't the oldest of the gang. My sisters were very young when our parents died in an accident, and Merry and I had to share responsibility for the youngest ones, though technically Merry was named their guardian. I'm also in the type of job that requires someone who's not hesitant about taking charge and having full responsibility. When guests have problems at an expensive hotel, it's the manager they demand to see. When the hotel isn't making enough money, the owners talk to the manager. So, yes, I suppose I have become a bit autocratic."

"A bit," Brooke agreed, emphasizing the understatement.

"What else?"

She blinked. "I beg your pardon?"

"What else?" he repeated patiently. "Is there anything else about me you dislike?"

"Well, I—" She couldn't really think of anything offhand, but then he'd caught her off guard. Lord, what a strange conversation!

"I'm not promising to change, Brooke," he went on when it was obvious that she couldn't answer his question. His mouth tilted into one of his boyishly appealing grins. "Like Popeye, I yam what I yam. But I'd make an effort to be less of a tyrant if you'd just give me a chance."

She raised a not quite steady hand to her throat, which was beginning to feel much too tight. Was he actually pleading with her to go out with him? Could he really want to be with her that much? Why? She'd certainly given him no encouragement. The word yes hovered on her tongue, but she bit it back, forcing herself to think clearly. He wouldn't change. Hadn't he said himself that it was highly unlikely that he would? Nor did she have the right to ask him to. But she could not— she *would* not—allow herself to become involved with him. She had too much at stake.

"I just don't think it would be very wise, Matt. I'm . . . I'm seeing someone else."

His eyes darkened dramatically, and she shivered at the suddenly hard line of his mouth. He had a real talent for looking intimidating, she thought ruefully. No wonder he was so good at his job. "You're talking about the guy you had lunch with that day?"

"Yes. Gary Wagner. We've been dating for several months."

"You're not in love with him, Brooke."

She moistened her lips nervously. "You heard the conversation. You know that I enjoy dating him primarily because I'm *not* in love with him. But I care for him."

"I care for my sisters, but I'm not interested in dating them," Matt countered scornfully."

"Gary is not my brother."

"He may as well be. Brooke, you're a woman of passion, of strong emotion. It's nothing short of criminal for you to tie yourself into a relationship that offers nothing more than mild affection."

Passion? Strong emotion? Startled by his description of her, Brooke was aware of a quick flare of panic. No. She'd worked very hard to control the more volatile side of her nature. She wouldn't be ruled by her heart or her hormones! "I really should be getting back now, Matt."

"Brooke, give it a chance. We could start by being friends," he urged.

Yes, he could talk her into being friends if she wasn't careful. He could talk her into just about anything if she let him. Brooke looked into his dangerously persuasive eyes and told herself that she'd be a fool to let him have even an inch. He'd be sure to grab a mile before she knew it. "I . . . I guess I don't need any new friends right now. Goodbye, Matt. Thank you for the lunch." She was out of the booth and headed for the door before he could stop her.

She expected him to follow her, to try to argue more. Instead he let her leave, just as he had that first time. She felt his eyes on her back until she closed Smitty's door behind her. It hadn't been a noble retreat, she told herself in disgust during the drive back to her shop. It had been an act of sheer cowardice, prompted by panic.

Still, she believed it was the smart thing to have done. And Matt was definitely the man to tempt her to be foolish.

JUST WHY *WAS* HE PURSUING Brooke Matheny when she'd made it quite clear that she had no intention of allowing him to catch her? Matt asked himself that evening as he wandered into the master bedroom of the elegant Amber Rose suite in which he lived. It wasn't that she was the most beautiful woman he'd ever seen. Her hair was thick, rippled in enticingly touchable waves to her slender shoulders that made him want to bury his face in it, but its glossy wheat color wasn't all that unusual. Her face was lovely, her brown eyes deep and expressive, her mouth designed to fit itself to a man's, but the features did not combine into exotically striking beauty. The body was good. Slim, of course, but not quite tall enough for model perfection. Not exactly voluptuous, but lithe and nicely proportioned.

Yet just the thought of her made him go weak with wanting her.

So, he mused, climbing into the huge, lonely bed in which he spent only a minimum number of hours to maintain his health, if it wasn't entirely a physical attraction, what *was* it? She hadn't exactly shown him the best side of her personality. In fact, she'd been downright bristly.

Yet he'd heard the affection in her voice when she'd talked to her friend Gary, and the shyness when she'd made her silly proposition to the poor man. He'd seen the passion in her eyes when she'd lost her temper with Matt. And he'd noted the way she'd smiled so sweetly at Smitty. God, he'd give his arm to have her smile at him like that.

"Fat chance," he muttered, arms crossed behind his head as he stared up at the darkened ceiling.

She didn't have the greatest opinion of him. Yet some instinct told him that she was as attracted to him as he was to her, though she was fighting it as hard as she could.

What would it take to reach her, to convince her that he wasn't such a terrible ogre?

She needed to get to know him better. Problem was, she wouldn't go out with him.

He'd have to go to her. One way or another, Brooke Matheny was going to have to acknowledge that Matthew James had entered her life and he wasn't going out of it without a fight.

He grinned in the darkness. If she actually thought he was going to give up so easily, she should have a little talk with his sisters.

HAUNTED BY IMAGES of leaf-green eyes asking for a chance, Brooke was unable to sleep that night. She got up after an hour of wasted effort and wandered into the living room of her apartment, where she spent the next couple of hours watching an old musical and working on the embroidered wall hanging she'd started a couple of months earlier.

"I want you, Brooke." The memory of his words whispered through her as clearly as if he were sitting on her couch beside her, murmuring into her ear. She shivered and closed her eyes, the embroidery needle halfway through the fabric in her lap. It wasn't hard to imagine making love with Matt. In fact, it was damned hard to stop herself from imagining it. Her heart raced, her mouth went dry, some feminine place deep inside her twisted with need. If he could do this to her with only his words—with only the memory of his words— imagine what would happen if he actually kissed her!

She'd already envisioned him bending over her, his mouth moving hungrily on hers, before she managed to shut out that picture. She groaned and opened her eyes, staring resolutely at the television set where Gene Kelly danced through the streets of Paris.

"I have to stop this," she said aloud, the fierce command aimed at her own traitorous imagination.

The problem was, she'd never particularly been tempted to make love with Gary. She'd convinced herself that in forcing the practical side of her nature to dominate her actions she'd become rather cold, eliminating more threatening emotions such as passion and desire. Now she knew that she hadn't eliminated all those emotions. It had taken Matt James to bring them to the surface. Sexy, handsome, arrogant Matt James.

Just thinking of him made her go weak.

She had to put him out of her life. She didn't try to kid herself that he'd given up after lunch that day. He'd try again.

She'd have to ignore him. He was a busy man. There were probably more accessible women begging for his attention. He'd get tired of being rejected eventually. Then he'd go away.

Trying very hard to disregard the depression that accompanied that thought, she scowled at the embroidery hoop in her lap and applied herself diligently to her hobby. It wasn't a very companionable way to spend her time, but at least it gave her something to do with the hands that seemed to beg her to allow them to bury themselves in Matt's thick, dark hair.

She might be able to ignore Matt, she told herself skeptically, but how in the world was she going to ignore her own hunger for him?

4

"IT'S FOR YOU, BROOKE." Rhonda's voice preceded her by only seconds as she stepped into the back room of the flower shop, her cheery, plump face creased with a broad grin.

"Who is it?" Brooke asked warily. As if she didn't already know.

"Guess."

Brooke sighed. "Tell him I died."

"He'd just order flowers for your funeral. And he'd probably insist on talking to you to do it. Now come on. Be a big girl and take your phone call."

Taking a deep breath, Brooke wiped the potting soil off her hands and stepped around the worktable to the telephone. She lifted the receiver to her ear and made an effort to sound cool and professional. "Brooke Matheny."

"Hi, Brooke."

"Hello, Mr. James," she responded briskly. "What can I do for you?"

He paused just long enough to let her know that there were several ways in which he'd like to respond to her question. "I need to order some flowers," he said instead.

Of course he did. He'd been ordering flowers every day for the past two weeks—ever since she'd cravenly run out on him at Smitty's. He refused to deal with anyone in her shop but Brooke, letting her know that the flower orders were nothing but an excuse to talk to her. So far he'd sent arrangements to his secretary, a hotel maid who'd had a baby, a guest of his hotel who'd been injured in a fall by the indoor heated pool, and had wired flowers to Missouri to one of his sisters—her birthday, he'd explained then. Brooke pulled an order pad in front of her. "What type of arrangement would you like?"

"It's such a fine spring morning. I thought I'd send something suitable to the weather. Jonquils, tulips, something fresh and springlike. You know?"

"Yes, I know," she replied repressively, jotting down his request.

"These are for a very special woman, so spare no expense. I want her to know for certain that I'm interested in her."

Brooke swallowed hard, trying to ignore a suddenly sick feeling somewhere in the pit of her stomach. She was *not* jealous, she assured herself firmly. Perhaps the doughnut she'd eaten for breakfast had been a bit stale. "Do you want these delivered, or will you be picking them up yourself?"

"Delivered."

"What would you like on the card?" She steeled herself as her fingers tightened on the pencil.

The line was silent for a moment; then he replied in a low, husky voice that curled her eyelashes. "'Gorgeous spring mornings and fragrant fresh flowers make me think of you. Anything beautiful reminds me of you.' Sign it, 'Yours anytime you want me, Matt.' Got that?"

Oh, God. Brooke looked down at the blank section on her order pad and hoped she'd remember the words she'd neglected to write down. Then she almost laughed, knowing his words were branded into her mind. "Yes, I have it. Where do we deliver these?"

"What's your home address?"

Brooke set the pencil down very carefully, counted to ten and then counted to ten again.

"Brooke?" Matt murmured when the silence stretched out. "Still there?"

"The flowers are for me?" she asked much too calmly.

"That's right. I know it's not particularly original to send flowers to a florist, but I'll try to be more creative next time. Now, about dinner tonight."

"There won't be a next time, Mr. James. And I'm not having dinner with you tonight!" This was the next step in his routine of the past two weeks—he would call, order flowers, then try to talk her into going out with him. So far she'd steadily refused all invitations. She had no intention of changing her answer this time.

"Brooke, when are you going to give up and go out with me?" Matt asked with good-natured exasperation.

"When pigs fly, Mr. James," she replied very sweetly, then hung up on his laughter.

"The man will not take no for an answer," she fumed to her avidly listening employee. "He's so arrogant that he thinks all he has to do is keep calling and I'll finally give in. He makes me so mad!"

"Honey, when *are* you going to admit defeat? You know you're dying to go out with him."

Brooke stared at Rhonda in openmouthed astonishment. "I'm— Have you lost your mind? What in the world makes you think I want to go out with that...that man?"

Rhonda laughed and shook her curly red hair. "Come on, Brooke, there's so much chemistry going on between you and that man that it's a wonder there hasn't already been an explosion. You only have to hear his name and your face turns red and your eyes start to sparkle and you get all excited. Admit it."

"That's called temper," Brooke snapped. "He makes me furious."

"He sure stirs up some kind of emotion in you. And I think that's great," Rhonda stated defiantly. "It's about time you started thinking about a man with your hormones instead of your head. Romance can't be planned out in that little appointment book of yours, Brooke Matheny. You can't fit it in whenever you have a few minutes scheduled for personal life. You don't go looking for a husband the way you scout out a new account for the florist shop."

Brooke threw up her hands in frustration. "Who said anything about marriage?"

"You have—several times. You've told me that you'd like to get married and start a family. Then when a perfectly eligible, fine-looking man comes along and shows an interest in you, you cut him cold. And how come, huh? Simply because it's the man taking the initiative instead of you? Because you didn't carefully select him for certain specified qualifications?"

"I don't understand why everyone thinks it's so terrible that I happen to think a lifelong commitment such as marriage should be based on serious, well-thought-out criteria instead of volatile, illogical emotions," Brooke complained, aggrieved at the lack of understanding from her friends. "One out of two marriages fails because the couple entering into the relationship didn't take the time to look at the long-range picture. They should have determined their common goals and interests, agreed upon the responsibilities each would accept for the maintenance of the union, drawn up budgets and financial aspirations, examined and minimized the areas of differing opinions or ambitions."

"I suppose you think they should also plan in advance how many times a week they'll make love?" Rhonda interjected dryly.

"If that happens to be an area of specific concern to either party, then yes, they probably should," Brooke retorted. "If more couples would use their heads instead of their hormones, as you put it, there would be a lot fewer failed marriages!"

"And a lot more extramarital affairs," Rhonda muttered.

"You, Rhonda Johnson, are an impossible romantic."

Rhonda grinned, undismayed. "Hey, what can I say? I certainly didn't marry Bud for his IQ or his bank account. I married him because I turned to Jell-O every time he kissed me, and we've been happily married for ten years and two kids. Sure, we've had our rough times, but we've made it through them—not because of any preexisting plan of action, but because we loved each other and didn't want to call it quits. *That's* what makes a marriage, Brooke Matheny."

Brooke leaned both elbows on the counter and ran her hands through her disheveled curls. "Wouldn't you at least concede that I should avoid the type of man that I already *know* I can't get along with? I can't bear a

bossy, overbearing male, and Matt James just happens
to be a Bossy, Overbearing Male—in capital letters. So
even without a great deal of thought and consideration, it stands to reason that a relationship between us
would probably be doomed, right?"

Rhonda laughed. "Uh-uh, kid. You're not suckering
me into that one. I still say you gotta give the guy a
chance before you can write him off. And you haven't
given him a chance."

"Nor do I intend to," Brooke said with finality. She
was quite relieved when the bell on the outside door indicated that a customer had come into the shop. Since
it was lunchtime, she and Rhonda were the only ones
working just then, meaning one of them had to go take
care of the customer.

"I'll go," Rhonda offered, turning to leave the back
room. "But don't consider the conversation finished,
Brooke. It's not!"

"It is as far as I'm concerned." Brooke turned back to
the arrangement she'd been working on before Matt
had called, taking only a moment to vent her frustration by ripping up the order sheet she'd filled out for
him. She had no intention of sending herself flowers
from him.

It had been a nice message, though, she thought reluctantly. If one liked all that mushy stuff, of course,
she added hastily before sternly turning her full concentration to her work.

"Okay, Carol, what else?" Matt asked patiently,
passing his secretary another signed report.

"That's just about— Oh, one more thing," Carol remembered, pulling several stapled papers out of the

stack of letters and reports in her arms and handing it to her employer. "This is from Clarice Fielding, the chairman of the local chapter of the National Heart Foundation. It's a letter thanking you for donating the use of the main ballroom for their fund-raiser this Friday, and a list of all the local business owners who have agreed to attend. I don't know why she sent you the guest list, unless she thought you might like to use it for future advertising of hotel facilities."

"That's probably the reason," Matt agreed. "Write her a note from me wishing her the best of luck with her fund-raiser, will you, Carol?"

"Yes, sir. Anything else?"

"Not now, thanks. Go to lunch."

She smiled. "Thanks. I'm starving. What about you? You're not going to skip lunch again, are you?"

He shrugged. "I'll grab something later."

Matt glared at the stack of paperwork on his desk— security reports, night audit revenue reports, reports from accounting, sales, housekeeping and catering, and the MOD—manager on duty—report from the previous night, among other matters waiting for his attention. He should have been through most of these first thing that morning, but he'd been greeted when he'd entered his office with several complaints from guests concerning room service problems during the previous evening.

After pacifying the guests with free breakfasts and abject apologies, having a long, stern talk with the room service staff and then handling a spate of calls that had come in for him, he'd barely had time for that quick call to Brooke before diving into work. He'd needed that call—funny how just a quick, not particularly encouraging conversation with her could perk him up. He'd chuckled for several minutes after she'd slammed the phone down in his ear. "I think she's weakening," he mused, then winced at his own optimism.

Matt sighed and reached for the first stack of reports, moving the papers from the Heart Foundation chairman out of the way. His hand froze on the papers when one particular name on the guest list caught his eye. He gazed impassively at the sheet for a moment, then a slow smile crossed his face. "Well, well," he murmured in satisfaction. "Looks like I'll be attending the fund-raiser Friday."

BROOKE HITCHED surreptitiously at the strapless bodice of her black dress, wishing she'd chosen to wear something else. Why, she wondered in exasperation at her own behavior, had she felt it necessary to dress to kill simply because she was attending a fund-raiser at the Amber Rose? True, it *was* a dressy affair, but she'd had several other choices of somewhat less seductive outfits, more suited to her wholesome, girl-next-door looks. She didn't even know why she'd come. Her first impulse upon receiving the invitation two weeks earlier had been to politely decline with a mailed contribution.

Still, she'd found herself taking a great deal of care with her appearance and coming anyway, telling herself that the contacts she would make would be good for her business, in addition to the donation she intended to make to the worthwhile charity. It wasn't that she'd expected to see Matt, she assured herself solemnly. She certainly hadn't dressed to impress him.

After all, she was making every effort *not* to encourage Matthew James, right?

So, her ruthlessly honest conscience taunted her, why was she aware of a rather hollow feeling of disappointment that Matt didn't seem to be in attendance at this party in his establishment?

"I don't believe we've met," said a smooth, rich male voice from somewhere close behind her bare left shoulder.

Brooke turned her head to find a tall, attractive blond male who matched the voice quite well. "No, I don't believe we have," she agreed with a friendly smile.

"I'm Dustin Chandler."

"Brooke Matheny."

Dustin Chandler held her hand for just a bit longer than necessary before releasing it with apparent reluctance. His bright blue eyes lingered for a moment at the cleavage exposed by the deep vee of her gown before he lifted them to her face, making her think that maybe the dress hadn't been such a bad idea, after all. The look in Dustin Chandler's eyes did wonders for her somewhat shaky ego. Her smile deepened as she found herself drawn into a lighthearted, pleasant conversation with the handsome man, who informed her that he was a single attorney who specialized in corporate law. Definitely an eligible male, she decided, wishing she could feel just a bit more enthusiasm at the thought.

MATT GLOWERED across the room at the couple in such animated conversation, their blond heads close together. *Too* close together, he fumed, watching as Chandler maneuvered himself a bit nearer to Brooke's slender body. Matt had planned to make his appearance earlier but had been detained by a problem with one of the guests. He'd entered the ballroom just in time to watch Dustin Chandler introduce himself to Brooke. Not that Matt was surprised that Chandler had singled Brooke out of the crowd. She was lovely tonight, her usually unruly curls tamed into a sleek knot at the top of her head, her excellent figure shown to perfection by the strapless gown.

He wasted a moment wondering why Brooke had never smiled at him the way she was now smiling at Chandler. Was it because they'd met in such an inauspicious way, embarrassing her because of the conversation he'd overheard? Or was it that Matt threatened her in a way Chandler did not? Made her less sure of herself, more aware of her own vulnerability? He wanted to believe the latter was the reason.

She was probably already checking out Dustin Chandler's qualifications as future-husband-and-father material, Matt thought morosely. Handsome, wealthy, successful. She'd probably already mentally added his name to her list of prospects.

And then Matt smiled, and anyone who knew him well would have observed that the smile was a dangerous one. Matt just happened to know one thing about Dustin Chandler—a man he'd met in several social situations. Chandler had one strict policy in his love life. And Matt knew what that policy was.

Chuckling beneath his breath, Matt headed across the room, his steps brisk with intent.

Brooke laughed at the joke Dustin had just told her and started to reply, but was distracted when a strong, unquestionably possessive arm settled around her bare shoulders. Startled, she turned her head to discover that the arm was attached to Matt James. Before she could recover from the breathtaking sight of him in evening clothes, he leaned over to kiss her lightly on her surprise-parted lips. "You can stop worrying about your kids, darling," he told her in a voice that carried clearly to the man with whom she'd been speaking. "I called the baby-sitter and she said to tell you that all four are tucked in for the night. The twins gave her a bit of problem at bedtime, but it's all taken care of now."

Without pausing to give her a chance to respond to the outrageous statement, Matt turned to Dustin. "Hello, Chandler. How's it going?"

The other man nodded, his formerly brilliant smile visibly dimmed. "Fine, Matt. How've you been?"

"No complaints." Matt smiled meltingly down at Brooke. "No complaints at all."

Brooke took a deep breath, fully prepared to let him have it regardless of the scene she might cause, but he stopped her with another quick, hard kiss. "Ready for that drink now, love?" he asked blandly.

Dustin Chandler murmured something that went unnoticed by the couple in front of him and faded into the crowd.

"Have you lost your mind?" Brooke asked through gritted teeth, the words very deliberately spaced. "What was that garbage about my kids?"

"Your four kids," Matt added, grinning without the faintest trace of apology. "I thought the twins were a nice touch, didn't you?"

Belatedly aware that his arm was still wrapped around her, Brooke tried to move away from him. His arm tightened, letting her feel the full strength of his lean, well-muscled body. She had to struggle to catch her breath. "Let me go, Matt." What should have sounded like a command came out sounding all too close to a plea.

"Well, at least you're calling me Matt," he observed, still without releasing her. "I wondered what it would take to make you stop calling me Mr. James."

"I'm going to call you several things if you don't let go of me right this minute," she promised furiously, trying to keep her voice low. "And then I'm going to call security."

He laughed. "Wouldn't do any good. The security guards all work for me, remember?" But he did release her then, letting his arm fall to his side, though he didn't step away from her.

Her first impulse was to run while she had the chance. Ignoring that ignominious urge, she lifted her chin and faced him squarely. "Now will you tell me what that little act of yours was all about? Why did you want Dustin Chandler to think that I have four children?"

"Very simple. He looked interested in you. He would probably have asked you out before the evening was over. I happen to know that Chandler makes it a policy never to date women with children. So I . . . misled him a bit."

"Misled?" she repeated scornfully. "You lied through your teeth."

He laughed. "That, too."

"And just what gives you the right to interfere in my social life?" she went on, ignoring the quivery feeling his laughter gave her. "Maybe I *wanted* Dustin to ask me out. He seemed like a very nice man. I was enjoying our conversation very much."

Matt shook his head, the soft lighting from crystal chandeliers glinting off his rich brown hair. "He's all wrong for you, Brooke. He has no intention of settling down to any one woman, and he doesn't like children. Not at all the right sort of husband for you."

Stung by his implication that she was still on the lookout for a husband, Brooke lifted her chin even higher, though she refused to allow herself to be drawn into an argument on the subject. "Thank you so much for your concern for my future," she said with icy sarcasm.

"No need to thank me," he returned smoothly. "My main concern about your future is making sure that I'm in it. I haven't told you yet how very beautiful you look tonight. You made my head spin when I spotted you from across the room."

Oh, Lord. Brooke swallowed hard against the sudden weakening that accompanied his softly spoken compliment. Had any other man ever looked at her in quite that way? she wondered wistfully, reading the unmistakable hunger in Matt's beautiful green eyes. She didn't think so. If only she weren't so certain that any relationship with him would end in disaster—for her, anyway. The man was a heartbreaker if she'd ever seen one.

"Come upstairs to my suite with me, Brooke," he murmured persuasively, reaching out to stroke her cheek with the back of one finger. "We can just talk, get to know each other better. I promise I won't ask any more of you—yet."

Oh, he was so very good at looking hopeful and sincere. Brooke could literally feel herself swaying toward him—and the sensation frightened her witless. "No, I . . . I—"

"Please, Brooke."

She lost herself in the warm depths of his eyes. Her mouth opened—later she would wonder if she would have said yes—but before she could speak, they were interrupted by a woman's high, artfully breathless voice. "Matt, darling! How nice to see you tonight. Clarice has been singing your praises all evening for the generous contributions you've made to the Heart Foundation. I told her that you are always a very generous man."

Brooke hated the buxom redhead on sight—something else that shook her badly. She wasn't usually so petty. She flinched when the redhead pulled Matt's head down for a kiss that looked particularly familiar. Matt's smile seemed a bit strained, but he spoke to the woman with impeccable politeness. "Hi, Heather. How have you been?"

"Lonely, darling," Heather answered with a pretty pout. *"Where* have you been?"

Matt laughed softly. "Busy. And don't tell me you've been pining away for my company. I hear you and Neal Lipton are quite an item these days."

Heather shrugged a peach-toned, perfectly rounded shoulder, covered only by the tiny spaghetti strap of her gold dress. "You know I'm not one to wait by the telephone, Matt."

"Hm." Without further comment on that subject, Matt turned. "Heather, I'd like you to meet a friend of mine, Brooke..." His words faded when he realized that Brooke was no longer standing beside him. There was no need to look for her. He knew very well that she was no longer in the ballroom. She'd run. Again.

"Oh, the pretty young woman you were talking to a moment ago?" Heather asked with just a touch of condescension. "She slipped away. I'm sorry. I didn't realize I was interrupting."

Matt shrugged with assumed nonchalance and changed the subject, though his fist clenched in the pocket of his hand-tailored slacks. Dammit, he'd been so close! He couldn't have misread the look in Brooke's eyes just before Heather had interrupted them. She'd been weakening, beginning to accept the inevitability of the attraction between them. Damn.

Not that he intended to give up now, he thought. If Brooke continued to run, he'd just pursue her more relentlessly. The more he saw of her, the more he spoke with her, the more he wanted her. And he'd never been one to accept defeat gracefully.

BROOKE SWORE as her blood stained a crimson dot into the partially embroidered fabric spread across her lap. Determining that the damage was not irreparable, she set the fabric aside, knowing she was in no frame of mind to concentrate on the tiny, intricate stitches. She leaned her head wearily against the back of the couch and closed her eyes. It was late and she should be in bed, but she couldn't sleep. Hadn't been able to rest since she'd gotten home from that ill-advised fund-raiser several hours earlier.

The moment her eyes closed, Matt's face sprang into her mind, as clearly as if he stood before her. She could still see the desire in his leaf-green eyes, the seductive, intimate smile on his firm, nicely shaped mouth. She could still feel that mouth on hers, reliving those two brief, hard kisses he'd given her for Dustin's benefit. Still feel his arm around her bare shoulders. His body pressed close to her side.

Groaning, Brooke opened her eyes and willed the images away. Not that she expected it to do any good. She knew she would be haunted by Matthew James that night—just as he'd haunted her from the day she'd met him. What was it about him that disturbed her so? she asked herself in bewilderment. She was always so firmly in control of her emotions, her behavior. No one else made her behave so unpredictably as Matt did.

And then she realized she'd answered her own question. Matt frightened her because of that very loss of control.

Brooke's success with Ribbons & Blossoms hadn't come easily. It had taken a major upheaval in her life before she'd even been able to take the first steps toward owning her own shop. Brooke Matheny had been born into wealth and power. Her life had been planned for her from the day she was born, the only offspring of a sweet, though pliable, mother and a strong, domineering father. Nathan Matheny had groomed Brooke from childhood to assume a role of leadership in his Denver corporation. He'd chosen her educational courses, hand-selected her friends and, later, her dates, encouraged her to spend her free time at his office "learning the ropes," as he often said.

Brooke couldn't pinpoint the exact date she'd claimed her independence. It had been a gradual thing, gaining strength as she'd begun to take a few courses of her own choosing in college, later reaching a peak after the painful discovery that her first serious love affair had been primarily based on the attraction of her father's money and position. At that time she'd been working for her father for two years and her future with his company was as clear to her as it was to everyone else. Nathan had her on a narrow, well-mapped path leading straight to the president's office. Brooke skidded to a halt on that path, breaking into a cold sweat at the thought of taking even one more step forward.

At twenty-three she'd finally found the strength to break away, moving to Nashville to start her own florist shop despite her father's bellows of outraged protest. She'd chosen Nashville because she'd fallen in love with the musical city on a college vacation. She'd taken with her only enough money to set up her business, deciding she'd earned it and it would be foolish to begin her new life with nothing.

During the past three years she'd planned her life as carefully as her father had ever organized it, but the glorious difference was that the plans had been her own. She was in control. She chose her goals, her friends, her dates. Keeping that control had become almost an obsession, extending even to her social life, resulting in her decision to enter a marriage founded on the same basic principles she'd applied to making her business a success. Matt James was the first person she'd met in three years who threatened her control. He'd burst into her life unannounced, uninvited, mocking her carefully laid plans, interfering with her punctiliously organized days. He made her feel unsure of herself again, vulnerable to the vagaries of emotion. He was arrogant, self-assured, unapologetically dictatorial. He hadn't been at all remorseful about ruthlessly interceding between Brooke and a man who was expressing an interest in her.

And, most frightening of all, he made her quiver with needs she'd held so very carefully under control for so long.

She wouldn't let him do this to her, she told herself firmly, swinging her feet to the floor and sitting up straight on the couch. She wouldn't let Matt James ruin her plans.

"'I am the master of my fate; I am the captain of my soul,'" she quoted defiantly aloud, remembering a line from Henley she'd had to memorize in high school.

And still Matt's kisses were the last thing on her mind when she finally fell asleep that night, the first thing on her mind when she woke the next morning. And not even a cold shower could completely dampen the heat those kisses had sparked in her.

5

BROOKE HAD JUST UNPACKED the last of the delicate porcelain dressing-table accessories she carried in her gift line when Christy Lovell, one of her part-time employees, called her to the telephone.

She hadn't heard from Matt for almost a week, not since running out on him at the fund-raiser. She'd begun to believe he'd given up and she'd told herself more than once that the rather hollow feeling in her stomach was nothing more than relief. So how come she was suddenly fighting down a rush of pleasure that he hadn't given up on her? Idiot, she called herself, even as she spoke to Christy. "Tell him I'm not here. Please."

Christy looked dismayed. "I'm sorry, Brooke. I've already told him you're here. It's Dr. Wagner."

Brooke relaxed, trying to make herself believe that she was *not* disappointed. Lord, what an idiot. "Oh, in that case, I'll take it. Sorry I snapped, Christy."

Christy smiled an acceptance of the apology before turning to help a customer. The shop had been quite busy that afternoon. Brooke made sure everything was running smoothly before lifting the telephone receiver to her ear. "Hi, Gary."

"Hi. Are you busy?"

"You know I'm never too busy to talk to you. What's up?"

"I thought I'd see if you want to grab a bite to eat tonight. I'm on call, so it may be another one of those dates that ends with me running out on you, but maybe we'll get lucky and finish an entire meal."

Brooke smiled. "I'd like that. Where do you want to meet?"

"How about Smitty's? I haven't had a Smitty Burger in months."

Brooke tried to come up with a plausible excuse to choose another restaurant. Failing, she sighed in resignation. "Yes, Smitty's is fine, Gary. What time?"

"Seven?"

"Okay, see you at seven at Smitty's."

Brooke hung up the phone, smiling faintly, and turned. Her breath caught hard in her throat. "What are you doing here?" she demanded in a voice that showed an annoying tendency to squeak.

Leaning negligently against the counter in front of her, Matt smiled. "I came to see you. Have lunch with me."

Brooke looked at her watch with an arched eyebrow. "It's one o'clock, Matt. I've already had lunch."

"Oh. In that case, have dinner with me tonight."

Relieved that he hadn't overheard her conversation with Gary, Brooke shook her head. "I already have plans."

"Tomorrow night, then."

"No."

"Brooke." Matt brushed absently at the lock of dark hair that fell over his forehead as he leaned farther across the counter, his gaze locked with hers. "Why?"

She sighed. Slipping her hands into the deep pockets of the pale yellow smock she wore in the shop, she wondered if she could make him understand. "You're a businessman, Matt. A successful one. Surely you understand hunches, instincts."

"Of course."

"Well, let's just say I have a hunch that going out with you would only lead to disaster. Maybe it's silly, maybe it's groundless, but I can't ignore the feeling."

"You still think I'm the man who can make you do something stupid."

She gulped at the reminder of their first inauspicious meeting. "Excuse me, Matt. I have customers to wait on."

He took her completely by surprise when he reached out to snag the back of her neck, leaned across the narrow counter and pressed his mouth to hers for a long, thorough kiss. Her first startled thought was of her customers and employees—it was so unprofessional to be kissed like this in the middle of her shop. Her second thought was that Matt kissed like an angel—or a devil. She was flushed and trembling by the time he released her, and neither reaction was entirely due to embarrassment.

"I'll be seeing you, Brooke Matheny," he murmured, his green eyes glinting with amusement at her discomfiture. And then he turned and strolled leisurely out of the shop, smiling and nodding at the others he passed.

"*That* was the man you've been trying to discourage?" Rhonda's voice asked from somewhere close to Brooke's side. "You need your head examined, boss. If I weren't a happily married woman, I'd be chasing him right now hoping to catch him on the rebound. What a man!"

Brooke glared at her broadly grinning employee, tossed her head in lieu of a reply—she didn't quite trust her voice just then—and turned with a firmly faked smile to offer her assistance to a woman who wanted a potted plant for a sick friend. It was a full half hour before she allowed herself to escape to the ladies' room, where she sagged bonelessly against the wall and fanned frantically at her face, which still felt suspiciously hot. As did the rest of her still not quite steady body.

GARY WAS WAITING for Brooke on the steps outside Smitty's at seven. "I saw you driving in right behind me," he told her, greeting her with a light kiss. "How was your day?"

"Nothing exciting happened," she lied with a smile, refusing to dwell on the inevitable thought of Matt and the kiss she'd been reliving all afternoon. "How was yours?"

"Long," he admitted. "And going to get longer. I've got a patient in the early stages of labor now. She's walking the halls of the hospital while I take a break to eat. Unless she does something dramatic or something else comes up, I should be able to finish a burger before I have to get back."

"Sure you don't want to give up medicine and go into your father's office-supplies business?" Brooke teased, knowing Gary would never willingly give up his profession. Despite the times she'd seen him suffer over losing patients, he loved being a doctor—even when it interfered with meals. Brooke had always admired his dedication. She'd have made a great doctor's wife, she thought regretfully, fully resigned now to never having more than friendship with Gary. But it was a close friendship, she reflected, smiling as she walked inside with him. One she would always treasure.

The receptionist was a young brunette with brilliant blue eyes and a skintight miniskirt. Brooke almost called her Lynette until she realized that it wasn't the same woman she'd met when she'd had lunch with Matt. Obviously Lynette had a sister. Introducing herself as Sherry, she led them to a table for two in a rather secluded corner perfect for quiet conversation with dinner. The other tables around them were being used for just that purpose, with the exception of the two empty tables on either side of the one where Brooke and Gary were seated.

Chatting idly with Gary as she studied the already familiar menu, Brooke paid little attention to the newly arrived diner settling in at the table closest to them, though she was aware of the movements around her. After all, Smitty's was a popular place. She couldn't expect total privacy. "I think I'll have the chicken strips with cherry sauce. And fries," she told the hovering waitress, blithely repressing a fleeting thought of calories and cholesterol as she set the menu aside.

"Excellent choice. I often have that here," proclaimed a cheerful, ominously familiar voice from that suddenly too close table next to them.

Brooke swiveled her head slowly, not at all surprised to find Matt grinning smugly at her from the chair where he lounged less than four feet away. "I'm glad you approve," she told him coolly, refusing to acknowledge that she'd ever seen him before. He *had* overheard her conversation with Gary earlier, she thought angrily, turning back to her companion with a grimace meant to express her disapproval of a stranger's impertinence. "What are you having, Gary?" she asked, keeping her voice low and steady.

Looking rather oddly from Brooke to Matt and back again, Gary hesitated for a moment before shrugging and placing his own order. "I'll have the Smitty Burger platter. Medium well. And a Coke. Want a Coke, Brooke?"

"A diet Coke, please."

"No need for you to count calories. You look great," Matt commented.

At Gary's quick frown Brooke shook her head. "Don't encourage him, Gary. Just ignore him. Maybe he'll *go away*," she added, stressing the latter two words.

"Don't count on it, sweetheart," came the quiet, amused reply from beside her.

The waitress who'd taken Brooke and Gary's orders returned for Matt's, greeting him by name. With Matt distracted by the necessity of answering the waitress, Brooke took advantage of the opportunity to start a conversation with Gary. "How's the little Jeffries girl doing, Gary? Is she responding to the new medication?"

Gary's smile answered her even before he spoke. "Yes, she is. She's showing significant improvement. Looks like we're going to pull her through."

"Oh, I'm so glad. I know how worried you've been about her."

He nodded, that familiar lock of dark red hair tumbling onto his broad forehead. "I've got to admit I was scared on this one, particularly when we'd tried almost everything and she still kept getting worse. I'm just grateful that we finally stumbled onto the right treatment. Infections like this in kids that small are damned tricky."

Though the waitress had gone to take Matt's order to the kitchen, he remained quiet at his table, for which Brooke was fervently grateful. Not that she expected it to last. He had to know that she was vividly aware of him sitting there, listening to her, watching her. She had the strangest sensation that she could hear him breathing, feel the warmth of his gaze on her. It took every ounce of her willpower not to look at him. Finding herself stroking her lower lip with one finger, as if she could still taste him there, she flushed and hastily dropped her hand.

Why was he doing this to her? she asked herself in near despair. And how much longer would she be able to hold out against his determined pursuit?

Realizing Gary was speaking to her, she forced herself to concentrate on his words, managing to make an appropriate response. They talked quietly about mutual acquaintances until the waitress reappeared with their dinners. Gary had made a sizable dent in his hamburger before he asked suddenly, "Hey, I forgot to ask. Did you get that new account you were hoping for? The Amber Rose Hotel?"

The bite of chicken strip she'd just swallowed tried to lodge itself halfway down her throat. Brooke could almost feel Matt sitting up straighter in anticipation of her answer as she forced the chicken down with a slug of her soft drink. "I haven't heard yet," she said when she'd set her glass down. "The hotel manager is a real crackpot. It's hard to tell just what he's going to do."

She knew she was flirting with danger, but rather than making a comment as she'd expected, Matt only laughed softly. Flicking another puzzled glance at the next table, Gary shook his head sympathetically. "Takes all kinds, I guess," he muttered, ostensibly in response to her comment, but including their pushy neighbor in the observation.

"Speaking of the Amber Rose," Gary went on after taking another large bite of his burger— Brooke had lost interest in her own dinner —"did you go to that Heart Foundation thing Friday night?"

"She sure did," Matt answered with apparent satisfaction. "Ever see her in that strapless black thing? She was a knockout."

Brooke choked and swung a furious glare at Matt, knowing he was repaying her for the crackpot remark. Hadn't she expected that he would?

"Brooke, do you *know* this guy?" Gary demanded, obviously holding on to his temper with an effort.

She turned back to him, reaching across the table to pat his hand. "Believe me, Gary, this man is totally strange to me," she answered flatly, without considering herself to be telling a lie.

Again Matt chuckled at the wording, seeming to find it amusing.

"Want me to complain? We can get the manager to take care of him," Gary offered.

But it wasn't necessary for Gary to call the manager. Smitty's voice boomed across the room as if on cue. "Matt! You ugly so-and-so, what are you doing back in my restaurant? I thought I'd gotten rid of you for a while."

"Hi, Smitty. The medium-well steak sandwich wasn't half bad tonight. I didn't even hear it moo when I bit into it this time."

Smitty's reply was cheerfully obscene, the slap on the shoulder he gave his young friend almost sending Matt to the floor. Brooke just *loved* watching this burly man assault Matt, she thought in satisfaction. Noticing her at the next table, Smitty's blue eyes widened in surprise. "Why, hello, Miss Matheny. How come you and Matt sitting at different tables this time? Was your last date so bad you couldn't bring yourself to repeat it?" he asked tactlessly, eyeing Gary in open curiosity.

"Brooke, you told me you didn't know him," Gary accused under his breath.

"I told you he was strange," Brooke corrected him irritably. "And, believe me, he is." She turned back to Smitty, gazing beseechingly at the grinning man. "Couldn't you hit him again, Smitty? For me?"

Smitty laughed. "I knew I was going to like you when Matt introduced you to me." The look he gave Gary was almost challenging as he added, "You come over to the house sometime with Matt, ya hear? The kids and me will help you keep him cut down to size."

Brooke managed not to groan at the blatant display of matchmaking. Despite Smitty's endless insults of Matt, he was obviously very fond of the younger man, and he'd decided Brooke was a suitable match.

"Dad, they need you in the kitchen," Sherry called.

Smitty nodded acknowledgement of the summons and then patted Brooke on the shoulder as he passed her, his touch considerably gentler than his usual cuffs at Matt. "See you later."

"Bye, Smitty," Brooke answered, avoiding Gary's eyes.

"I could've told you Smitty would be on my side," Matt told her, managing to sound a bit sympathetic.

"Would someone mind telling me just what's going on here?" Gary asked mildly.

Matt stood, walked the few steps to their table and offered his hand to the other man. "Hi, I'm Matt James—the crackpot manager of the Amber Rose Hotel. You must be Brooke's friend, Dr. Wagner. Nice to meet you."

Caught off guard, Gary shook the proffered hand, his hazel eyes narrowing on Matt's face. "You look familiar."

"I've eavesdropped on you and Brooke before," Matt replied jovially. "The day she proposed to you. Remember?"

"I think I'm going to be sick," Brooke groaned, hiding her face in her hands.

Beginning to find the humor in the bizarre episode, Gary asked only, "You knew each other then?"

"No, we met afterward. Have you ever tried Smitty's cheesecake?" Matt asked unexpectedly. "It's fantastic."

"No, I haven't, but it sounds good. Would you like to join us for dessert?" Gary asked politely.

"Gary!"

Gary only smiled broadly at Brooke's wail of protest. "What else can I do, Brooke? He's obviously not going away."

Matt had already pulled his chair around to the table for two, the resulting crowdedness putting him thigh to thigh with Brooke. She scooted as far away from him as possible, her leg tingling from that brief contact. Her action seemed only to amuse him further. She wondered if the watery remains of her soft drink dumped into his lap would dampen his humor a bit. Only her dread of causing a scene kept her from trying to find out. Then again, she told herself glumly, he'd probably find that funny, too. A man with Matt's nerve, a nerve strong enough to allow him to unrepentantly crash her date with another man, probably wouldn't be at all embarrassed at having a drink dumped in his lap in a public place.

Both Gary and Matt seemed to find a great deal to amuse them during the next fifteen minutes or so. By the end of that time Brooke was ready to drown both of them. Laughing at something Matt said, Gary grinned at Brooke. "You know, I kind of like this guy," he announced.

"Fine. *You* date him," Brooke muttered.

"She really is a very nice person," Gary told Matt gravely. "Great sense of humor, sweet personality, soft heart."

"Yes, I know," Matt assured him, causing Brooke to throw him a startled look at the sincerity in the answer. How could Matt claim to know any of those things when she'd been prickly and defensive with him since the day they'd met? she wondered almost wistfully. And, darn it, she *was* all those things! So why did she always turn into a shrew in Matt's presence?

For the first time since she'd known him, Brooke was dismayed when Gary's pager called him away from dinner. "That must mean Mrs. Gianelli has decided to have the baby," he murmured, shutting off the high-pitched beeping. "Sorry, honey."

Brooke managed to smile. "That's okay. I hope everything goes well."

"I'm not expecting any problems." He leaned over to kiss her cheek, then shook Matt's hand. "Nice to meet you, James."

"You, too, Wagner," Matt returned solemnly, his eyes shining with his smile. "We'll probably be seeing more of each other."

Gary looked from Matt to Brooke, grinning broadly. "Oh, I'm sure of it."

Brooke reached for her purse as soon as Gary was gone. "As delightful as this evening has been," she said with not-so-subtle sarcasm, "I really must be going."

"I'll see you home."

"Thank you, that's not necessary. I have my own car."

"Then I'll follow you."

"No."

"Brooke." Matt placed his hand on her arm, seeming not to notice when she flinched at his warm touch. "We have to talk. Let me follow you home now and let's talk awhile. When we're finished, I promise you if you ask me to get out of your life I'll do it. Believe me, my ego has just about had all the rejection it can take from you."

She eyed him warily. "You swear it? You'll stop hounding me if I let you have your say tonight?"

"If that's what you want."

She believed him. "All right."

His fingers stroked a light caress as he pulled them away. "Thank you."

As she climbed into her car, she fervently hoped she wasn't making the biggest mistake of her life.

BROOKE LOCKED her car door and turned to appreciatively examine the low, sporty vehicle parked in the space next to hers. Matt climbed out of the fire-engine-red sports car, ducking under the gull-wing door, which opened upward.

"What kind of car is that?" she asked him, tilting her head to study the sleek lines.

"A 1968 Porsche Carrera 6," he answered with such boyish pride that she nearly laughed. He ran a hand almost reverently over one raised fender. "Isn't she gorgeous?"

"Yes," Brooke answered honestly, "she is."

"Maybe you'd like to go for a ride in her sometime?" he offered tentatively.

Since she had every intention of asking him to get out of her life for good, she didn't answer, concentrating instead on digging her apartment keys out of her roomy purse.

"Nice," Matt approved when they were inside her living room.

"Thank you," Brooke answered, wondering how the room had suddenly gotten smaller. "Could I get you anything? Coffee? Something stronger?"

"No, thanks." Matt sat on the flowered chintz sofa, lifting her partially finished needlework from its resting place in one corner and studying it closely. "This is beautiful."

"Thank you." Brooke took a chair halfway across the room from him, crossed her legs and nervously smoothed her straight skirt over her knees.

"Did you do the one on the wall, as well?"

She glanced at the framed cross-stitch view of a blue jay surrounded by apple blossoms. "Yes."

"You're very good. One of my sisters—Marsha— enjoys needlework. She's always got some project going."

"You told me you have four sisters?" Brooke asked, latching on to the innocuous subject even though she knew she was procrastinating.

"Yes." He smiled at her in a way that told her he knew she was putting off a more serious discussion about their own relationship but was willing to allow it for now.

"Do you have any nieces and nephews?"

"Merry and Grant have a three-year-old son, Lucas, and they're expecting another child in a few months. Marsha and Tim have eighteen-month-old twin daughters—guess it runs in the family."

"You must have very hectic reunions," Brooke commented.

He laughed. "Yeah, but we have fun. How about you? Any brothers and sisters?"

Brooke shook her head. "Only child."

"Are your parents still living?"

She remembered him telling her that his own parents had been killed. How hard it must have been on the young family to lose their parents so abruptly, she thought sympathetically, then felt guilty about the rift between her and her own father. "Yes, they live in Denver."

"You're from Denver?"

"Yes. I moved here three years ago to open my flower shop."

"Why Nashville?"

She shrugged. "I'd visited here and I loved it."

He nodded understandingly. "It's a great town. See, we have that in common, Brooke."

"Living in the same city is hardly a sufficient basis for a relationship," Brooke pointed out, knowing her stalling was at an end.

"It's a start," he replied. "Who knows, we may find lots of other things in common if we give it a chance. Look how easily we've been talking for the past few minutes. Why don't we try it again—say, tomorrow night over dinner?"

"Oh, Matt."

"I know, you have a feeling that we'd be disastrous together. Well, *I* have a feeling that we'd be great together. So why don't we compromise?"

She eyed him suspiciously. "Compromise?"

"Yeah." Gaining enthusiasm, he leaned forward, clasped hands resting between his knees as he attempted to sell her on his idea. "Give me one month. If at the end of that time you're still convinced we're all wrong for each other, all you have to do is say the word and I'm history. What do you say?"

"Just what would this month include?" she asked cautiously.

He didn't even hesitate. "Nothing you don't want it to include. We'll spend time together, go out on regular dates, get to know each other better. Find out if we have anything but a strong physical attraction going for us."

She tilted her chin at his rather immodest implication that she was strongly attracted to him, but declined to call him on the statement. After all, it was true. Obviously they both knew it. "All right. You've got a month. But I warn you, I'm a busy woman. I'm not guaranteeing any minimum number of free evenings during the next month to spend with you."

"Fine. I'm busy myself. We'll work it out as we go along. You won't be sorry, Brooke."

"I think I'm already sorry," she murmured, grimacing ruefully. "I should be furious with you for crashing my date with Gary tonight, and instead I'm agreeing to go out with you."

"'Desperate times call for desperate measures,'" Matt quoted with a crooked grin.

"I think that should have been, 'Arrogant men employ arrogant measures,'" Brooke corrected just a bit too sweetly.

He shook his head reprovingly. "Brooke, is that any way to start a relationship?"

Relationship. A sudden spurt of panic brought her out of the chair and to her feet. "Well, Matt, it's been an . . . interesting evening."

He rose slowly. "Does that mean it's over?"

"That's right." She moved purposefully toward the door.

"It's still early."

"I'm tired."

"You'll see me tomorrow night?"

She held the door open. "Yes."

"I'll pick you up here. Seven o'clock okay with you?"

"Fine." She was beginning to get desperate to be alone to think. "Good night, Matt."

He stopped only a few inches away from her. "Good night, Brooke." And then she was in his arms and his mouth was on hers. Dazed by the suddenness of his move, she belatedly remembered how quick he could be. And then she forgot to think at all as she lost herself somewhere in the depths of that devastating kiss.

If Brooke hadn't already suspected that Matt was like no other man she'd ever known before, her response to his kiss would have told her so. No one had ever affected her this way. Her senses shut down, closing out all sound, all sight, all awareness of anything but Matt's lips on hers, his tongue expertly tangling with hers. Her body flared out of control, her pulse racing, her legs weakening, her skin burning everywhere he touched, her breasts swelling against his solid chest. She'd been kissed many times, but never like this. *Never* like this.

His face buried in her hair, Matt continued to hold her even after he finally released her mouth to allow her to breathe. His arms were tight around her, cradling her snugly against his lean, unmistakably aroused body. Her knees still weak, Brooke could only cling to him, her eyes closed as she tried to bring her breathing under control.

Matt finally drew back, though his hands remained on her shoulders as if to steady her—or himself. She opened her eyes and stared mutely up at him. "Brooke..." he began, then stopped, touched her cheek with one finger and stepped away. "Good night," he told her. And then he was gone.

Brooke closed the door behind him, then leaned weakly against it for a long moment before she found the strength to walk to the couch and collapse onto it. She sat stiffly for a time, then groaned loudly and fell sideways, hiding her flushed face in a lace-edged throw pillow. She'd made a *big* mistake agreeing to this next month, she told herself sternly.

THE COLD SHOWER TOOK the edge off Matt's physical discomfort, but his mental condition was something else. He'd thought he'd known how badly he wanted Brooke Matheny. He'd thought what he felt for her was desire, coupled with the pleasure he found in her company, even in their heated sparring. He hadn't expected what should have been a routine good-night kiss to escalate into something so shattering, so momentous that it would force him to completely reevaluate his feelings for her.

He'd believed that his main fascination with her had been in the challenge she'd presented. No insatiable womanizer, Matt had practiced discrimination in his former liaisons with women, choosing to become intimate only when genuine respect and affection were present. Still, it had been a long time—if ever—since he'd been forced to chase any woman as diligently as he had Brooke.

The thought of a lasting, serious relationship had never been distasteful to him; just the opposite, in fact. He'd always assumed that someday he'd find a woman with whom he'd want to spend his life, start the family he'd like to have. He *hadn't* expected to have her suddenly enter his life and turn it upside down. That thought drew him up short, making him freeze in the process of pulling a white T-shirt over his still-damp head. Was Brooke that woman? Brooke, whose ideas of marriage were ridiculously pragmatic, downright cold, in fact? Brooke, who had resisted and defied him since their first odd meeting? Brooke, who had responded so passionately to his kiss even as she'd tried to convince him that they were all wrong for each other?

He grinned suddenly. Brooke Matheny just might be the one he'd been waiting for, the only woman in his future. And he'd persuaded her to give him a month to convince her that he just might be the one man in hers. He was whistling when he walked out of his bedroom in search of a late snack. The next month would have to be handled very carefully on his part. The possible outcome was simply too important for carelessness.

6

RIBBONS & BLOSSOMS WAS awarded the Amber Rose account the day after Brooke agreed to go out with Matt for one month. Skeptical at first, she realized after talking to the purchasing manager that Matt had exerted no influence on her behalf, trusting her to get the account on her own merit. She was grateful that he hadn't interfered. She would have hated not knowing whether he'd given her the account as a bribe for her to be "nice" to him. Not that she would have put it past him, she assured herself hastily, unwilling to be too generous to Matthew James.

Brooke was surprised, to say the least, when the delivery man arrived at Ribbons & Blossoms later that day with a narrow white box usually associated with long-stemmed roses.

"He's sending you flowers from another florist?" Rhonda asked in surprise, looking puzzled as Brooke stared at the box on the counter in front of her.

"I told you he was strange," Brooke answered, knowing without having to read the card who'd sent the gift.

"Aren't you even going to open it?"

Brooke sighed and pulled off the gold ribbon tied around the box. She lifted the lid and gave a startled laugh. He *had* sent her long-stemmed roses. *Chocolate* roses. A half dozen in assorted flavors—two each of milk chocolate, dark chocolate and white chocolate. Had he known or had he only guessed that Brooke adored chocolate?

Rhonda sighed enviously as she looked into the box over Brooke's shoulder. "Godiva—expensive candy. Lord, they look sinful," she added, ruefully patting her well-rounded hips.

Murmuring a distracted response, Brooke lifted out the card, steeling herself for a blatantly seductive message. The card held only two words, in a bold, masculine handwriting that had to be his own. "Love, Matt."

She swallowed hard. Love? Since when had that word come into this . . . relationship? she finished for lack of a more applicable word. Matt wasn't in love with her any more than she was in love with— Oh, heavens, she thought with a mental groan. She wasn't falling for him, was she? Surely she couldn't be that reckless!

No, she decided abruptly. She wasn't in love with Matt James. She wouldn't allow herself to be. And he wasn't in love with her. He probably tossed the word around as easily as he did the orders he gave to his staff. He'd made it quite clear that he was out to seduce her and he'd use any weapon in his arrogantly male arsenal to do so. Including chocolate roses.

Before she went back to what she'd been doing when the delivery arrived, she carefully tucked his card into her purse so it wouldn't get lost, refusing to think about her reasons for doing so.

"BROOKE, WOULD YOU RELAX? I'm not going to jump you right here in public, I swear." Matt's low voice was half amused, half exasperated.

Flushing guiltily, Brooke squirmed in her seat. "I didn't think you were," she muttered, not quite truthfully.

"Then loosen up. You're so tense I'm afraid you're going to hurt yourself."

Brooke took a deep breath and tried to relax, as he'd suggested. She didn't know what had gotten into her. She'd been this way ever since Matt had picked her up at her apartment. It was as if she were so certain something would go wrong that she felt she had to prepare herself for any eventuality. *You're being an idiot*, she told herself in disgust, prying her fingers loose from the strap of the purse she held in her lap as they waited for the play to begin.

Matt had somehow obtained tickets for a performance of *Cats*, part of the Broadway Theater Series held in the Tennessee Performing Arts Center—known as T-PAC to natives of Nashville. Though familiar with the music, Brooke had never actually seen the production. She greeted the dimming of the lights with an anticipation that went further toward easing her tension—so much so that she didn't even jump when Matt leaned close enough that his arm pressed against hers during the second act. During the performance she was able to completely lose herself in the music and the dancing, forgetting to worry about the risks of spending too much time with Matt. During intermission she remembered, and she found herself stiffening again, to her exasperation as well as his.

She found herself humming "Memory" as she rested comfortably in the low leather seat of Matt's Porsche, idly staring out the window at the passing scenery as they made the short drive to Printer's Alley, where they would eat a late dinner at Boots Randolph's.

"Nice song, isn't it?" Matt asked, his voice slipping softly into the quiet in the car.

"Beautiful. One of my favorites," she admitted.

"Mine, too. So you did enjoy the performance?"

"Very much," she assured him, surprised that he felt it necessary to ask. She twisted on her seat, straightening the skirt of her garnet silk dress around her knees as she faced him. "Didn't you?"

"Sure. I love plays and musicals. I hold season tickets to the Broadway Theater Series and I spend a lot of evenings at T-PAC or Starwood," he said, naming a popular amphitheater. "I even like community theater. I took some drama classes in college, even thought briefly of becoming an actor."

"Really?" She was surprised and didn't bother to hide it. "Why didn't you?"

He shrugged. "I'd just begun to realize that I had more ambition than talent when my parents were killed. After that, well, it seemed too frivolous, I guess. I went into a steadier career that would pay well and leave me enough free time to help out whenever I could with the twins."

Again Brooke wondered how drastically Matt had been changed by his parents' deaths. Had he always been so supremely self-controlled, so briskly competent? she wondered. Or had those traits been forced upon him when he'd unexpectedly found himself the oldest male member of a young, devastated family?

After a rather awkward beginning they chatted easily enough over dinner until Brooke suddenly found herself noticing that candlelight did fascinating things to Matt's handsome face. The flickering illumination danced across the smooth planes and angles of his cheeks and jaw, reflected in tiny pinpoints from his exotic eyes, brought out glistening highlights in his thick brown hair. She didn't even realize that she'd stopped talking to simply stare at him until his expression changed and his eyes locked hungrily with hers. The sudden sensual awareness made her flush darkly and look quickly at her plate. She was fervently grateful to Matt when he smoothly picked up the threads of the conversation they'd been having earlier, as if that highly charged moment had never occurred.

They lingered over dessert as they enjoyed the music of "Mr. Yakkety Sax," Boots Randolph. Brooke was always disappointed when he wasn't performing on a night when she ate at his supper club. Inevitably it came time to leave. She found that her hands were trembling again when she reached for her purse. Chiding herself impatiently for the ridiculous manner in which she'd been acting most of the evening, she lifted her chin in an unconsciously regal gesture and swept out of the club at Matt's side.

"I've had a lovely evening, Matt," she said when he'd pulled his car into a parking space outside her apartment. Intending to leave him sitting behind the steering wheel, she reached surreptitiously for the door handle. "You needn't—"

"Save it," he interrupted shortly, opening his own door. "I'm coming in."

He was out before she could protest and had her door open before she could do so herself. Ducking her head beneath the door, she slid out of the low car and stood, automatically straightening her skirt. "Matt, I—"

"I said save it." He turned and walked toward her apartment, gripping her forearm as he walked to almost pull her along with him. Something about the jerkiness of his usually graceful movements, the set of his firm jaw, made her think he was angry with her. Why?

She started to try again to dismiss him when they'd reached her door, but a glance through her lashes at the expression on his face kept her prudently quiet. He *was* angry. There was no mistaking it. And she knew him well enough by now to know that there would be no dismissing him until he was quite ready to leave. Acknowledging defeat, she unlocked the door as he stood silently waiting.

Inside the apartment, she tossed her purse on a chair and turned to face Matt, who'd remained standing and was towering over her, glaring at her. "All right, let's have it," she challenged him. "What's your problem?"

"*My* problem?" he repeated incredulously. "You want to know *my* problem?"

"Yes. You're obviously angry. Why?"

"Damn right I'm angry." He shoved one hand through his dark hair, the other into the pocket of his tailored gray slacks. "You agreed to give me a month, Brooke. One month of dating and spending time together, getting to know each other better, finding out if we might possibly have a future together."

"I know what I agreed to," she answered defensively, her arms crossed tightly in front of her. "And I'm living up to it, aren't I? Didn't we just spend an entire evening together?"

His short laugh was not amused. "Oh, we sure did. An entire evening of you pressing yourself against the door of my car, looking at me as if I were an ax murderer and you my next victim. Every time you almost forgot to act like a cringing coward and started to enjoy yourself, something reminded you and you went back into your shell. Just what the hell have I done to make you act that way with me, Brooke? You damn sure don't look at Wagner like that when you're out with him. I know, remember?"

She could almost believe she'd hurt him. Disgusted with herself, unaccountably annoyed with him for making her face her foolish actions, Brooke dropped her arms and sighed. "You're right. I'm sorry."

He looked at her suspiciously, as if expecting something more. "That's all?"

"What else can I say? You're right. I behaved like an idiot this evening, and I'm sorry. I don't really know what made me act that way. It was just—"

"Just what?" he prodded, his voice becoming less hard, more gentle.

"You . . . you make me nervous," she blurted out without thinking, then blushed because she'd sounded like a silly, gauche teenager.

Matt didn't laugh at her confession. Instead, he stepped even closer and put his hands up to cradle her face. "What are you so afraid of, Brooke?" he asked, his voice pure seduction.

Her heart beat crazily in her throat, almost blocking her voice. "I . . . I don't know."

His head lowered slowly until his lips just brushed hers. "This? Is this what frightens you?"

Her lips trembled beneath his, mutely answering his question.

Her eyes had drifted closed, so she didn't see his smile. But she felt it curving his lips against hers. "Don't be afraid, sweetheart. Don't ever be afraid of this. Or of me."

And then the smile was gone and his lips were taking hers with all the hunger she'd seen in him earlier, all the passion that lay behind the sparkle in those deep emerald eyes of his. Brooke could only moan softly and cling to him as she plunged with him into swift currents of desire that carried her away from everything she'd known before. This is what she'd been afraid of, she acknowledged with what little clarity of thought he left her. Each time he kissed her it was like nothing she'd ever experienced. Each time was more incredible, more shattering. More addictive. Brooke could grow much too dependent on his kisses. And already her body craved more. Ached for more. Burned for more.

As if sensing her need to be touched, or perhaps responding to his own desire to touch her, Matt's hands swept her from shoulders to hips, learning her curves, pressing her snugly against his own lean frame. She could no more have stopped her hips from pressing into his bold arousal than she could have stopped her blood from pounding in her veins. The intimate contact made Matt groan deep in his chest and hold her even tighter, his tongue plunging repeatedly into her mouth even as his hips mimicked the erotic rhythm.

Just before it would have been too late for either of them to call a halt to the lovemaking, Matt drew back, his body shuddering its protest. "Tell me to stop, Brooke," he ordered, his voice so raw it was nearly unrecognizable.

"Stop," she whispered obediently, though she longed to call the word back, to beg him to go on.

"All right." He released her after making sure she was steady enough to stand on her own—though barely—and stepped away from her, shoving an unsteady hand through his uncharacteristically disordered hair. His eyes held hers captive. "I'll always stop when you ask. Never be afraid that I won't."

She didn't know what to say, so she said nothing. After a moment he moved to touch her again, then clenched his fist and hurriedly backed away, as if not quite trusting his own willpower to keep his promise to her. "Good night, Brooke. I'll call you tomorrow."

He'd just opened the door when she stopped him. "Matt?"

He stiffened, looking warily back over his shoulder. "Yes?"

She moistened her kiss-swollen lips. "Are you sure you don't want to forget our agreement? I mean, our first date wasn't exactly a success. By the end of the evening, you were furious and I—"

"You promised me a month. I'm holding you to your word." His tone encouraged no argument. He gave her no chance to respond before he'd stepped outside and closed the door behind him.

As usual, he hadn't asked what *she* wanted, Brooke thought resentfully, staring at that closed door. He was going to hold her to her promise whether she liked it or not. And, being a woman of her word, she'd cooperate. But only to a point, she told herself with fierce determination. She'd go out with him occasionally during the next month, but she would not go to bed with him. If his kisses had the power to destroy all the control she'd worked so hard to obtain during the past three years, she could only imagine what his lovemaking would do to her. And she would *not* fall in love with him! She simply would not.

And then she closed her eyes and prayed for strength as she trembled again in the aftermath of his kisses.

TWO WEEKS PASSED before the next confrontation. Two weeks of tentative, progressively more relaxed outings to dinner, the symphony, more plays and local productions. Two weeks of kisses that went just to the edge of insanity before one or the other of them managed to find the strength to pull away. Two weeks of telephone calls that stretched long into the night on those evenings when they couldn't see each other, calls during which they gradually learned more about each other. Their likes, dislikes, political views, religious philosophies, childhood memories.

Brooke told Matt that she'd like someday to own an entire chain of florist shops; Matt admitted that his dream had always been to own his own vacation resort, adding that he'd already found someone who shared his interest and that the two had been discussing the idea of opening a resort close to Nashville. At Matt's urging, Brooke told him a bit about her falling out with her father; he made little comment, but she could tell he'd filed her words away for future reference. He talked about his family, and his love was apparent in each word he spoke about them.

Though he made it quite clear that he hadn't stopped wanting her, he didn't press her to go to bed with him, for which she could only be grateful. If he had pressed, she wasn't sure she would have had the willpower to resist. Each kiss she shared with him was as spectacular as those first mind-spinning kisses. She found herself craving more of them, more of his touches.

She hadn't realized that she'd fallen into the habit of letting Matt know her plans for each day until one particular Friday, two weeks after their first date, when he let her know quite graphically that he'd begun to expect her to do so.

It had been an especially busy day. Two of the local high schools were holding their proms that evening, which meant a rush of corsages and bouttonnieres, and the daughter of a faithful customer was being married, which meant that Brooke and several of her part-time employees spent most of the afternoon decorating the church. Just as they'd finished, the young bride, nervous to the point of near hysteria, tearfully decided she'd chosen the wrong colors for the ceremony. Brooke and the bride's mother had managed to convince her that the colors were lovely and the decorations spectacular, but it had taken time and patience.

Brooke barely had time to rush home and change for the baby shower she was attending for a woman who'd been her friend for two years, since they'd met through a professional organization they both belonged to. She thought briefly of calling Matt, but she was running late, and after all, they didn't have a date for that evening.

The shower was a big success, attended by a large group of women of around Brooke's age, most of whom she knew. If she was aware of an occasional twinge of envy during the evening when she looked at the happily married expectant mother's radiant smile and admired the tiny garments and soft blankets displayed on the gift table, Brooke managed to ignore them and have a marvelous time. They had such a good time, in fact, that the party didn't break up until quite late. It was after eleven when Brooke entered her living room, exhausted, but pleasantly so.

She'd just crawled into bed when the telephone rang. "Hello?" she asked, somehow knowing it was Matt.

"Where the hell have you been?" he barked, his anger carrying quite clearly through the telephone lines.

Brooke held the phone away and stared at it for a moment before bringing it back to her ear. "I beg your pardon?"

"I've been calling you all day. You weren't at the shop. And you haven't been home all evening. Where were you?"

Her own temper igniting, Brooke sat straight up in bed and tossed back her hair. "That is none of your business, Matt James," she told him heatedly. "I don't have to account to you for my time."

"Maybe we need to make something clear," Matt said in return, enunciating each word with deadly precision. "When you agreed to give me a month, you were agreeing to an exclusive arrangement, whether you were aware of it or not. I was willing to be patient when your work kept you from going out with me, but I'll be damned if I'll sit meekly at home while you go out with other men!"

"Nobody asked you to!" She threw back the words, her knuckles going white with her fury that he'd condemned her without a trial. "And I did *not* agree to any sort of exclusive arrangement with you, Matt. I simply said I'd go out with you a few times during this month. If that's not agreeable to you, then we'll end it right now."

"Oh, you'd like that, wouldn't you?" His voice had risen to the point that she held the receiver an inch or so from her ear. "You've been looking for a reason to call off our agreement from the very beginning. Well, it's not going to work, Brooke. You gave me your word and you're not backing out, understand? I've got two more weeks of your precious time, and I'm going to fill those weeks so full that you won't have time to even *think* of another man, much less actually go out with one. Your search for the perfect husband will just have to wait for another couple of weeks!"

He hung up with a crash that made her wince.

"Ooh! That . . . that— Ooh!" Brooke sputtered, slamming her own receiver into its cradle with enough force to make it jingle protestingly beneath her hand. She couldn't think of any word despicable enough to describe Matthew James. How dare he call her and scream at her in that way? How dare he treat her as if he owned her?

"Exclusive arrangement, indeed," she muttered, jumping out of bed to pace off some of her fury. When that didn't work, she looked for something to throw. Lacking anything more satisfying—anything she didn't mind breaking, that is—she snatched her pillow off the bed and slammed it against the wall. She couldn't remember ever being this angry, not even at her father. Which only went to prove that she never should have gone out with Matt James in the first place. Hadn't she known he'd do this to her? Hadn't she known he'd take her well-ordered life and turn it completely inside out?

"He wants his two more weeks," she snarled aloud. "All right, Matt, you've got them. I keep my word. And then you can just jump in the nearest pond for all I care. It's an appropriate place for a frog!" Satisfied with the word she'd finally found to describe him, she stormed into the kitchen to vent the rest of her rage on a huge bowl of chocolate ripple ice cream.

THE GLASS HIT THE WALL with a thud, splashing the remainder of the drink liberally on the carpet. Matt was only sorry the glass hadn't broken. He'd meant for it to break. He was furious. Not with Brooke—though he was still plenty mad at her—but mostly with himself. He'd mishandled that phone call. Badly mishandled it.

He'd be lucky if she'd ever even talk to him again, much less go out with him during the next two weeks. After all the work of the past couple of weeks, all the patience, all the cold showers, he'd blown everything with one stupid phone call. She'd finally come to trust him a bit, to relax enough to talk candidly with him, even to seem to to trust him a bit, to relax enough to talk candidly with him, even to seem to enjoy his company. And then he'd screamed at her like a maniac and given her orders like a two-bit dictator. Great going.

His only excuse was that he'd been calling her for the past ten hours. Never a man of patience, Matt's had been growing progressively thinner until finally it had snapped. By the time she'd finally answered the phone, sounding sleepy and content after putting him through hell as he'd wondered who she was with, what she was doing, he'd been ready to attack. And he had.

It wasn't that he hadn't meant everything he said. He had no intention of allowing Brooke to waste any of the month he'd wheedled out of her by dating other men. It was just that he could have found a more tactful way of letting her know if he'd managed to control that temper of his.

Which made him remember Brooke's temper. Lord, she'd been mad. He didn't even want to think of how furious she'd be when she discovered that he wasn't about to allow her to break off their budding relationship at the end of the month she'd granted him, though he knew full well she'd try to do so. The past two weeks had served only to deepen his fascination with her, and he wouldn't let up until she was his. Until she stopped fighting him and acknowledged that she was his.

Still cursing his ill-judged tantrum, he wandered into his kitchen and opened a cabinet door, pulling out a bag of Oreos. He had to do some serious thinking about the best way to repair the damage he'd done that evening.

The thought that the damage could be irreparable never even occurred to him.

BROOKE WASN'T QUITE SURE how to greet Matt when she opened her door for their Saturday-evening date, which had been arranged several days earlier. They hadn't spoken since the telephone quarrel the night before, so she half expected a continuation of the fight. Instead, Matt greeted her with a smile and a swift kiss, hustled her out the door before she had a chance to say much of anything, asked her to listen to a new rock tape he'd just bought that day and used the volume of the tape player in his car as an excuse to delay discussion.

She realized he was deliberately avoiding any chance of a serious conversation when he took her to a loud disco restaurant for dinner. The fried shrimp and oysters were delicious, but the decibel level of the music playing in the background required them to practically shout to be heard. "Matt, this is ridiculous," she almost yelled at him when they'd finished eating.

He grinned. "Wanna dance?"

She just managed not to roll her eyes. "Why not?"

Brooke almost laughed aloud when, the moment they stepped onto the dance floor, a slow, quiet song began to play. So much for Matt's brilliant strategy to evade conversation, she thought smugly, stepping into his outstretched arms. "Well?" she asked after they'd been dancing for only a moment.

"Well, what?" he inquired, his mouth close to her ear. Too close, she immediately decided, squirming a bit in the intimate clasp of his arms.

"I'm still waiting for an explanation—and an apology—for that telephone call last night. You had no right to—"

"You're absolutely right, and I apologize," he interrupted quietly, one hand slipping lower at her waist.

Trying to keep her mind on the conversation while her spine seemed to be turning to applesauce, Brooke cleared her throat. "And the explanation?"

"No explanation. Just an apology."

She frowned and tilted her face up to look at him, refusing to let him off that easily. "Matt, why did you—"

The words lodged in her throat when his mouth covered hers. He kissed her slowly, thoroughly, without stopping his seductively rhythmic movements in time to the sensual beat of the music. She'd never been kissed on a crowded, dimly lit dance floor. She'd had no idea it could be so totally erotic. Unconsciously she pressed closer to him, feeling him harden against her. Some tiny, still rational part of her mind attempted to remind her that she was angry with this man, but for the life of her, she couldn't remember why. Her fingers tightened at his waist.

The deejay saved her from thoroughly embarrassing herself by playing a loud rock song almost before the slow dance had ended. Jarred into reality by the discordant change, Brooke jerked back, realizing that it wouldn't have taken much more to have her pulling Matt down to the dance floor. Lord, what magic did this man wield over her?

"Let's get out of here," Matt growled in audible frustration, his hand gripping her arm as he led her to the exit. Mutely, still stunned, she allowed him to propel her outside. He reached for her the moment they'd settled into his car, and she was in his arms again, their mouths moving hungrily together, tongues thrusting eagerly, bodies striving to overcome the physical limitations of the small sports car. His hand slipped beneath her soft white sweater to stroke the heated flesh of her waist, then inched upward toward one straining, aching breast. Brooke almost groaned in anticipation.

Again the interruption was abrupt and jarring. A hand slapped against the roof of the Porsche, the thud accompanied by raucous laughter and mercifully unintelligible suggestions from the three young men passing the car. Cursing beneath his breath, Matt reached for the door handle, but Brooke stopped him with a hand on his arm. "Let's just go, Matt. Please."

He released his breath in a hard gust and pushed back the hair that had fallen onto his forehead. His eyes glittered feverishly when he looked at her, his cheekbones flushed with the heat of his passion. "All right. I'll take you home," he said at last, his voice grating huskily.

The drive to her apartment was short and silent. Matt parked, then jumped out of the car to open Brooke's door for her. He helped her out with a hand at her waist, closed the door, then pushed her back against the car as he kissed her again and again. Drugged with the increasing intensity of those kisses, Brooke could only cling to him and return them. Finally he drew a shuddering breath and pulled back, turning her in the circle of his arm to walk her to her apartment.

Brooke's hand was trembling too hard to fit the key into her lock. She handed Matt the key, gratified to note that his own fingers were not quite steady as he unlocked the door. "Would you...would you like to come in for coffee?" she asked when he'd returned the key ring. She wasn't sure that inviting him in was such a bright idea, considering the way the evening had been going, but she couldn't seem to help asking.

He hesitated, then cupped her face in his hands, looking down at her. "If I go into your apartment now, I won't be leaving until morning," he told her roughly. "Is that what you want?"

Her eyes widened. "No, I—"

"Then I won't come in." He managed a crooked, rather painful-looking grin. "I don't seem to have any willpower against you tonight."

She swallowed hard, knowing how shaky her own willpower was where Matt was concerned. "I— All right."

He started to move away, then turned and caught her in his arms for one last hug. "Brooke, the next two weeks...let them be mine. Please. Only mine."

"Oh, Matt," she said with a sigh, knowing she'd never be able to resist him when he said please. The word seemed so foreign to him.

"Two weeks, Brooke. No other men for two weeks. Is that so much to ask?"

"There won't be any other men, Matt," she said, conceding defeat. Would there ever be another man who'd make her feel this way? she wondered in a sudden rush of near panic.

She couldn't quite read the expression that crossed his face. Gratitude? Satisfaction? Victory? Before she could analyze it, it was gone, replaced by a knee-melting smile. "Thank you. I'll call you tomorrow, okay?"

"Okay." She turned as he began to walk away, then some unexplainable impulse made her turn her head and speak to him. "Matt, I spent yesterday afternoon decorating a church for a wedding. Last night I went to a baby shower for a friend. All women. We had so much fun that we didn't break up until late."

Matt froze at her words, then turned rapidly and started toward her. Brooke was inside her apartment, the door closed behind her, before he could reach her. She sagged backward against the door when she heard him walk away again after a long pause. Why? she asked herself furiously. Why had she told him? Had she no sense of self-preservation? Didn't she know that he'd take her explanation as an acknowledgement that he'd had the right to know?

"Oh, Matt," she moaned, hiding her face in her hands. "What are you doing to me?"

SHE NEVER QUITE REGAINED her equilibrium during the following two weeks. Matt seemed to make sure that she wouldn't, changing from one date to the next, one time a perfectly behaved, courteous gentleman, the next an ardent, eager lover just barely held under restraint.

Rhonda teased Brooke mercilessly about her frequent daydreaming spells, her erratic mood swings, her sudden, seemingly inappropriate smiles. "Still trying to convince yourself you're not crazy about this guy?" she asked one afternoon when she'd caught Brooke again staring absently into space, her hands frozen around a half-finished flower arrangement. "Is this the face of a woman in love?"

Annoyed, Brooke flushed and bent her head back to her work. "Don't be ridiculous. Of course I'm not in love with Matt. Besides, his month is almost over. Tomorrow night marks the end of it. After that, I don't plan to see him anymore. I've kept my bargain."

"Just like that, huh?" Rhonda made no effort to hide her amused skepticism. "You're just going to stop seeing him."

"I think it's for the best," Brooke agreed. "He and I are too . . . well, he's turned my life upside down, Rhonda, and you know I don't deal well with chaos. Once I stop seeing Matt, things will be back to normal. Just the way I'd planned."

Rhonda shook her head in visible disgust. "You still think you can plan romance, don't you? Even after the past month."

"I still think it's better to remain in control of one's emotions, yes," Brooke answered defiantly. "Speaking of Matt," she went on, determinedly changing the subject, "did you send Gerry over to check the lobby plants at the Amber Rose? I'm sure it's about time to rotate them with fresh ones from the greenhouse."

"Yes, she's there now," Rhonda replied, silently acknowledging that the subject of Brooke's relationship with Matt was closed. For now. "Oh, and you need to call Mrs. Delaney again. She's three months behind on her bill this time."

"All right, I'll do that as soon as I'm finished here. We know she'll pay; she just has to be prodded a bit."

"That's why I'm letting you do the calling. I get too annoyed with her procrastinating. You're nicer than I am."

Brooke smiled and turned back to her work as Rhonda went into the other room. Her smile faded as soon as she was alone. It wasn't going to be easy to break off with Matt, she thought. He wasn't going to take the rejection easily. And she had to admit—if only to herself—she didn't really want to stop seeing him. But she had to. Before she got even more deeply involved with him than she already was. Before she made the drastic mistake of falling in love with him, putting her so carefully planned future into his hands, taking the risk that he would eventually destroy her. Yes, she was being a coward, and yes, she knew it, but wasn't that better than putting herself in danger of having her heart slashed?

She only hoped that her life *would* get back to normal when Matt was no longer in it. Would she stop thinking of him constantly, longing to be with him, waking in the night trembling after another erotic dream of him? Of course she would, she told herself bracingly. Out of sight, out of mind, right?

Matt called later, just as she'd decided to get ready for bed. She knew that he'd been in meetings that evening with the out-of-state owners of the Amber Rose, and she could hear the weariness in his voice. "Tough meetings?" she asked sympathetically.

"Long," he answered. "The Amber Rose is running smoothly, but the owners like to look for weaknesses anyway. Almost as if they have to justify the expense of making the trip here."

Brooke had a hard time imagining Matt answering to anyone. "When do you think you'll be able to start on your vacation resort and become your own boss?"

"Oh, Ken and I are still talking about it, but we have to come up with the capital. There's a lot of paperwork and research to be done first to be used to tempt investors."

Brooke thought of her father, who'd often been known to invest in just such fledgling undertakings, particularly if he had faith in the courageous entrepreneurs behind the ideas. His shrewd instincts and daring investments had made him very rich during the past thirty years. Something told her that her father would consider Matthew James worthy of his consideration. They had so much in common, after all. Two hard-headed, ambitious businessmen with a great deal of confidence in their own talents and abilities. Brooke reluctantly admitted to herself that she had a bit in common with them herself; she'd known all along that her father would have invested in her business, despite his reluctance, had she asked him to. But she'd wanted to do it on her own, to prove her own worth, her own competence.

"Brooke? Still there? You haven't fallen asleep, have you?" Matt asked teasingly, reminding her that she'd drifted off into her own thoughts.

Brooke responded lightly, telling herself not to be silly. She had no intention of putting Matt together with her father. Introducing him to her parents was hardly the best way to stop seeing him, she reasoned.

"Where would you like to go tomorrow night?" Matt asked after they'd talked for a few minutes longer.

She swallowed, knowing what lay ahead of her the next evening. "I, um, it doesn't really matter."

"Do you like Gayle Malone?"

The increasingly popular new country-pop singer was one of Brooke's favorites. "Very much. Isn't she performing in your lounge this weekend?"

"Sure is. How about dinner here and then we'll catch her act? I'll introduce you to her if you'd like to meet her."

"That sounds like fun."

"Oh, by the way, all the local hotel managers have been invited to a reception at our major competition—the Opryland Hotel—on Sunday afternoon. It's a PR event for Opryland—their way of making sure we guide our guests in the park's direction. Sounds like it's going to be quite a big shindig. Want to go with me?"

Sunday. Had he forgotten that the next night—Friday—marked the end of his month, or was he so confident that Brooke would want to keep seeing him? Not that she'd given him any indication that she didn't enjoy his company, she admitted to herself. Matt couldn't know that the more she found herself liking him, the more determined she was to regain control of the situation. "We'll, uh, we'll talk about it tomorrow, okay?"

Matt was quiet for so long that she wondered uneasily if he'd read her thoughts. She wasn't ready for the confrontation yet, she thought nervously. Not over the telephone. She almost sagged in relief when he said only, "All right. We'll talk about it tomorrow. I'll pick you up at seven."

"Why don't I just meet you there?" she suggested. "There's no need for you to come after me when we're only going back to the Amber Rose." Besides, that way she'd have her own car in which to make her escape after telling Matt that she wasn't going to date him anymore.

He seemed about to argue, then changed his mind. "Fine. I'll wait for you in my suite."

"At seven, then."

"Yes. Good night, Brooke. Sleep well."

The latter two words were said in a low, husky, intimate tone that made her shiver. She managed a coherent response, then disconnected the call, knowing that her night would be a restless one, disturbed by dreams of Matt.

SHE WAS GOING TO END IT, Matt thought, glaring down at the telephone on the table beside him. During the past month Matt had learned a great deal about Brooke Matheny. And he knew now that she was going to end it. Had known from the moment she'd hesitated when he'd asked her to the Opryland affair on Sunday.

He clenched his fist and slammed it against his knee. Why was she doing this to them? Couldn't she see that whatever they had was too important for her to just turn and walk away because their feelings were too intense for comfort?

His jaw set in determination, he paced restlessly around his suite. He wouldn't permit it, dammit. He wouldn't allow her to blithely send him on his way. He'd been so careful to restrain himself with her, to hold his desire for her in check until she was ready to acknowledge that the feelings were mutual. He'd taken more cold showers during the past few weeks than he had since he'd been a hormone-tormented teenager, and still she refused to acknowledge that she wanted him as badly as he wanted her. But he knew. Her responses to his kisses hadn't lied, nor had her eyes in those unguarded moments when he'd caught her looking at him with so much longing that it had been all he could do not to throw her over his shoulder and carry her to the nearest bedroom.

He wasn't leaving her life without a fight. He wasn't going to allow her to break it off until he'd forced her to admit that she was as deeply involved as he, and he'd make her acknowledge that she was running from that involvement because she was afraid. Then he'd show her that she had nothing to fear from him. That he'd never willingly hurt her. That they could make magic together.

"You're mine, Brooke Matheny," he said out loud, savoring the words, no longer surprised by the unfamiliar possessiveness this woman brought out in him. "By this time tomorrow, you'll know it as well as I do."

BROOKE STOOD STIFFLY outside the door of Matt's suite, smoothing her cream silk dress and wondering if she'd dressed correctly for telling a man she no longer wanted to see him. She'd taken extra pains with her appearance that evening and knew she was looking her best. Perhaps she only wanted to leave him with an attractive picture of her, she decided, trying to smile at the thought.

Remember the plan, she told herself in a mental chant. *Remember the plan* Cool, calm, collected. Friendly but firm. She hadn't actually rehearsed her speech to him, but she knew exactly what she intended to say. "Matt, you said that if at the end of one month I still thought our dating was a bad idea, you'd accept my decision without argument. I'm holding you to your word, just as you've held me to mine for the past month."

Perfect. She reached up to knock lightly on the door.

She knew the moment she looked up and saw his face that the evening wasn't going to be as easy as she'd hoped. Something about the set of his firm jaw told her that Matt was not in a manageable, agreeable mood. But then, when had he ever been? she asked herself in wry amusement.

"Come in, Brooke," he said, stepping aside to allow her to enter the suite.

She'd never been in his suite before. She'd very carefully avoided that. She walked in somewhat warily, her gaze darting around the tastefully luxurious decor before fixing on the table for two set up in the center of the huge living area. "We're eating here?" she asked unnecessarily, taking in the crisp white linen, elegant place settings, candlelight and flowers flanked by silver-covered serving dishes.

"Yes. You don't mind if we serve ourselves, do you? I wanted privacy."

She gulped, wanting to tell him yes, she did mind, but unable to do so. Though what she had to tell him was best said in private, it suddenly seemed too soon. She'd hoped for dinner in the restaurant downstairs, accompanied by quietly innocuous conversation, followed by an hour or so of Gayle Malone's show, after which she would quickly tell Matt that she didn't want to see him again and then make her escape as swiftly as possible afterward. She should have known Matt would foil her plans. He was making sure that the confrontation would come quickly, with no outsiders to distract them.

He knew, she thought without surprise. He knew what she planned to do. And he wouldn't make it easy for her.

Dinner was superb, of course. Medallions of veal, steamed vegetables, an excellent wine that probably cost more than her monthly phone bill. He was definitely not making it easy for her. Brooke picked at her food with little enthusiasm, barely tasting the dishes that she would have deemed heavenly at any other time. She answered Matt when he spoke but, for the life of her, could think of nothing original to say.

"This is ridiculous," Matt said when one silence had gone on for several long moments.

Startled by his words, grated out in a low, angry voice, Brooke dropped the fork she'd been using to push food around her plate. "What?"

He tossed his linen napkin onto the table and stood, jerking his chin toward the sofa. "Let's get it over with."

"But . . . I'm not finished with my dinner," she protested weakly, spurred by sheer cowardice.

"No, and at the rate you're going, you won't be finished until next Tuesday. Come on, Brooke. Tell me what you came here to say."

Sighing defeat, she rose and followed him into the conversation group made up of the low, comfortable-looking sofa and two conveniently arranged armchairs. She started to perch on the edge of one chair but was forestalled by his hand on her arm. "Over here," he ordered, guiding her not so gently to the sofa. "Sit."

Whether he'd planned it or not, his imperious command stiffened her spine and loosened her previously paralyzed tongue. Tossing her head in defiance, she sat. "I don't appreciate being pushed around, Matt."

His lips twisting into a grim smile, Matt sat beside her, turning to face her fully. Brooke eyed that smile warily, wondering what she'd said to amuse him.

Matt wasn't amused, exactly, but he *was* pleased that he'd managed to spark her temper. He hadn't known how to deal with the nervous, uncertain, almost frightened woman who'd sat across from him at dinner. *This* was the Brooke he'd come to know. Brave, defiant, challenging him to stay ahead of her. He wanted her passion tonight, and if temper proved the catalyst, then he'd start with that. He kept his voice stern. "All right, spit it out. Tell me why you didn't want to talk about doing something together on Sunday."

Her huge brown eyes narrowed in resentment at his tone. "Maybe you haven't been keeping track of the time since our first date, Matt, but I have. You asked me to give you a month, and I have. You might say that tonight marks our anniversary."

He'd thought he was ready to hear her break it off— or *try* to break it off. It seemed that he wasn't. He interrupted before she could go on. "Has the past month been so terrible?" he asked her, unable to conceal the hint of vulnerability in the question.

Her face softened almost imperceptibly. "No, Matt," she answered in little more than a whisper. "It hasn't been so terrible."

He shifted closer, one hand lifting to toy with a wheat-colored curl resting on her shoulder. "We've had fun, Brooke. We've never been at a loss for words with each other. We have so many interests in common."

"We also both have fiery tempers that we seem to set off in each other," she reminded him defensively. "Don't you remember the fight we had two weeks ago?"

His fingers moved from her hair to the soft hollow behind her ear. "Yes, we have tempers. And we're going to lose them at times. Surely you don't expect to find a relationship in which there is never a disagreement. Not only is that impossible, it would also be incredibly dull."

"You enjoy quarreling?"

"No." With satisfaction he felt her involuntary shiver when his fingers slipped down to stroke her throat. "I don't enjoy quarreling. But it's inevitable between two hot-blooded, strong-willed people."

"Exactly," she agreed as though she'd made a point with his words.

"Two people whose passions are as hot as their tempers," he went on softly, as if she hadn't spoken. His other hand went up to cup her face between his palms, and he lowered his head to nibble gently at her lips. "Who have only to touch each other to go up in flames."

"Matt," she moaned, her eyelids drifting downward as he pulled her into his arms without taking his lips from hers. "Don't do this."

"I have to, Brooke," he muttered rawly. "God help me, I have to." And then his mouth pressed fully against hers so that neither of them could say more.

He'd kissed her many times during the past month, but he'd always held something back, knowing the embraces would go no further. This time he kissed her as he'd wanted to kiss her from the first time he'd seen her, with everything he had to give. His tongue was insistent, insatiable, sweeping the inside of her mouth to claim every centimeter for his own. His hands were equally busy, moving hotly over her slender curves, lingering here and there to stroke, press, tease. Brooke shifted restlessly in his arms, then seemed to give up fighting him. With a broken little sob of need, she pressed closer, offering all of herself to him, her tongue meeting his and then initiating a foray of its own.

She wasn't going to stop him this time. Matt's shoulders relaxed in relief even as other parts of him hardened almost painfully. He shifted, his weight bearing her down into the deep cushions of the sofa. Brooke gave a little sigh and tilted her head back to give him access to her neck as his lips searched out the hollow of her throat. He wondered what was going through her mind just then. He knew she wanted him. Was she giving in to her desire only to satisfy her curiosity before sending him on his way? The thought bothered him for a moment, but then her hands slipped into his hair as she arched beneath him and all rational thought fled.

The tiny buttons of her cream silk dress opened easily to his unsteady fingers. Pushing the fabric aside, he discovered the lacy camisole she wore beneath. Already aroused, her nipples pushed upward through the flimsy material, demanding his touch. He lowered his head to nuzzle one swollen peak, dampening the fabric covering it. And then he opened his mouth to take her deep inside, fabric and all, his tongue and teeth working the hardened nub until her fingers clenched into fists and her breath came in harsh, ragged gasps. Only then did he ease the camisole down to expose her bare breasts to his hungry eyes.

"So beautiful," he muttered, burying his face in the lightly scented valley between those soft, perfectly shaped mounds. "So damned beautiful."

Brooke's hands stroked his back through the jacket of his dark suit. "I want to touch you," she murmured, plucking discontentedly at the fabric.

"I want you to touch me," he replied, lifting his head so that their eyes met. "Just as I want to touch you. Everywhere. Make love with me, Brooke."

She hesitated for only a moment, but her decision had been made during that first kiss. "Yes, Matt. Please."

Growling his satisfaction with her response, he swept her off the couch and into his arms, turning without pause to move toward his bedroom in long, impatient strides.

8

BROOKE LOOPED ONE ARM around Matt's neck as he carried her, her free hand going to the knot of his tie. By the time he set her on her feet beside his bed, she had the tie loosened, as well as the shirt button beneath. She allowed no doubt to shadow her pleasure in touching him; she had made her decision and she would not change her mind. She didn't have to analyze her reasons for making love with him. She'd known from the moment she'd heard the vulnerability in his question about whether she'd enjoyed the past month that she would not be able to carry through with her original plans. The words she'd needed to break off their relationship had died in her throat. She knew now that she wouldn't say them.

Sometime during the past month Brooke Matheny had fallen in love.

She hadn't wanted to admit it; she'd fought it as fiercely as she could. But when she'd looked in Matt's eyes and realized that she held the power to hurt him with her words, she'd known her struggle had been in vain. Hurting him would have been hurting herself.

Her gaze meeting and holding his, she slipped the jacket off his shoulders, letting it fall unnoticed to the floor. Without blinking she began to unbutton his white silk shirt. When Brooke Matheny conceded defeat, she surrendered wholeheartedly, she thought in a flash of wry humor.

Matt stood very still as she eased her hands beneath his shirt and pushed it off to join his jacket on the floor. He drew in his breath sharply when her hands slid slowly from his shoulders downward, lingering at the points of his aroused nipples before moving down his hard stomach to pause at the waistband of his slacks. He had a beautiful body, she thought in delight. Hard and lean and tanned. His chest was sleek, glistening, smooth, his arms subtly roped with strong muscles. She had never seen a more beautiful example of masculinity.

Though his muscles quivered beneath her touch, Matt made no move to help or hinder her. Instead, he watched her with those intense, expressive green eyes, almost daring her to continue.

Her smile felt decidedly feline even to her. Her fingers never hesitated as she unbuckled his belt and released the snap of his slacks, carefully easing the zipper downward to relieve the strain of his arousal. If Matt needed proof that she would be a willing participant in their lovemaking, she'd give him that proof. Her hand slipped inside the opening of his slacks.

Matt groaned and tugged her into his arms, holding her firmly against him. His low laugh was uneven and a bit hoarse. "Ah, sweetheart, if you only knew how badly I've wanted you during the past weeks. I don't know how much control I've got left."

"Show me how much you want me," she challenged him, wriggling out of his arms to drop her partially unbuttoned dress to the floor to join his discarded clothing and her shoes, which she'd kicked off without noticing.

She could almost feel Matt's gaze on her as his eyes moved slowly down her briefly clad body. Wearing only the lacy ivory camisole, a matching half slip and sheer panty hose, she stood proudly before him, warmed by the approval she saw on his face. She had never felt more feminine, more attractive. She lifted a hand to one camisole strap.

"No," Matt muttered, stepping forward to cover her hand with his. "Let me."

It took him only a matter of minutes to strip her out of her clothing, and less than that to remove his own. And then, very slowly, he pulled her toward him.

Brooke let out a shaky sigh of pleasure when she finally found herself held full-length against him, nothing at all between them. He was so warm. She rubbed sinuously against him before pressing closer to flatten her swollen breasts against his hard chest. His legs were long and rough to her smooth ones, his arousal full and hot against her stomach. She wanted him with an intensity that astonished her. She'd never known such hunger before. "I want you, Matt," she told him, barely recognizing her own voice.

The sound he made could have been a laugh or a sob. He moved, her world tilted, and then she found herself on her back beneath him on the bed. His mouth and hands moved ravenously over her, lingering in one place only long enough to bring incredible pleasure before moving to accomplish the same purpose elsewhere. Brooke gasped and arched into his touch, her head spinning at his abrupt transformation from tenderness to desperation. His breath was hot on her thigh, and then his lips moved inward, causing her to cry out in startled wonder.

"I can't—I can't wait any longer," he groaned, surging up her body to bury his face in her throat.

There was no need for him to wait. She tried to tell him so, but her voice was thick, her words inarticulate. She told him instead with her hands and her half pleading, half demanding movements. Grasping his lean buttocks, she urged him to continue. Remembering at the last moment to ask her if she was protected from pregnancy, Matt rose swiftly, his thrust taking him deep inside her.

Insanity. Hunger. Swirling colors splashed on mindless darkness. Broken words and ragged gasps. Pleasure so intense it bordered pain. And, finally, a shuddering explosion of light and sound, followed by quivering weakness. Brooke lay limply in Matt's arms, full consciousness returning so slowly that she wondered how long they'd been lying there, recovering. A thin film of sweat covered them both, cooling her skin where it was exposed to air. She shivered and pressed closer to him.

"Are you cold?" Matt asked, his voice husky with the remnants of passion.

"Uh-huh," she murmured, uncertain of her voice.

He reached down to pull the hastily discarded comforter over them both, tucking it tenderly around her bare shoulders. "Better?"

"Uh-huh."

He laughed softly. "Are you going to sleep?"

"Uh-uh," she answered, shaking her head. And then she snuggled more deeply into his shoulder, closed her eyes and slid without resistance into a deep, dreamless sleep.

WHEN SHE WOKE, she was alone in the bed. Blinking her eyes against the dim light provided by a small bedside lamp, Brooke turned her head to find Matt sitting in a nearby chair, wearing only a pair of jeans. His expression was sober, distant, his thoughts obviously far away. He hadn't noticed that she was awake.

Brooke cleared her throat. "Matt?"

His head jerked around, his face clearing instantly, deliberately. "Hi."

She smiled. "Hi. I guess we missed Gayle Malone."

"Yes. It doesn't matter."

Rising to one elbow, she tucked the comforter over her breasts, tilted her head and regarded him quizzically. He was acting strangely. Surely he wasn't regretting what had happened between them. Or... And suddenly she thought she knew what was troubling him. He still thought she was going to end their relationship.

"Matt, about that reception at Opryland on Sunday. I'd love to go with you."

She'd expected him to smile. At least to look pleased. Maybe even smugly victorious, knowing Matt. Instead, he frowned and surged restlessly to his feet, his hands deep in his pockets as he half turned away from her.

"Matt?" she asked when he didn't say anything. Wrapping herself as best she could in the oversize comforter, she climbed out of the bed and stepped closer to him. "Matt, what's wrong?"

Though he still refused to look at her, he did finally speak. "When you came here tonight, you planned to break it off, didn't you? You were going to tell me that my month was over and you didn't want to see me anymore."

"Yes, I was," she admitted quietly. "I changed my mind."

Only then did he turn to face her, his emerald gaze drilling into her. "Why?"

Why? She mentally groped for words, wondering how to answer him. She knew the reason, of course. She was in love with him. But she wasn't ready to tell him, didn't know if he wanted to hear it. She wasn't even sure he'd believe her yet. "I don't want to stop seeing you," she said at last, settling for that small part of the truth.

"Brooke, I—" He stopped, ran a hand through his mussed dark hair and began again. "I knew what you were going to say tonight, and I didn't want to hear it. So I, uh—"

"You seduced me," she finished for him, amused at the guilty look on his face. "You distracted me with sex. And now you think I'm so overwhelmed by your incredible lovemaking that I no longer know my own mind."

He scowled, his lean cheeks going suspiciously pink. "I wasn't going to put it quite like that."

She laughed softly. "Matt, I know what I'm saying. I've fought it for the past month, but you've won. You were right when you said I wouldn't be able to walk away from the attraction between us. If I hadn't already come to that conclusion, I never would have made love with you. Believe me."

His frown lightened, his eyes gleaming with an expression that looked a lot like hope. "You really don't want to end it?"

"I really don't."

"You no longer believe that some terrible disaster will come from our being together?" he pressed.

She hesitated. How could she answer that one? As it happened, she *did* still believe that their affair could only end in pain. She wasn't expecting happily-ever-after for her and Matt, but she intended to take whatever pleasure she could find in their relationship until it ended.

Matt's frown returned, pulling his dark brows sharply downward over his narrowed eyes. "You do, don't you? You still think we're doomed to some sort of tragic breakup. Brooke—"

She didn't want to talk about the end. Not now. Deliberately letting the comforter fall to her feet, she stepped forward and wound her arms around his neck, bringing her breasts into contact with his bare chest. "Must we waste time discussing the future when we have tonight all to ourselves?" she asked in her most seductive voice.

Matt inhaled deeply. "Now you're the one using sex as a distraction," he accused her, though his hands went swiftly up to hold her more snugly against him.

"Yes. Any objections?"

His hesitation was hardly noticeable. "No," he groaned, lowering his head to hers. "No objections."

She smiled against his mouth. "Good," she murmured before he took away her ability to speak.

"GLENN, THIS IS MR. ANDERSON," Matt told the Amber Rose driver, motioning toward the weary traveler beside him. "His luggage has been misplaced by the airline, and he's stranded here without a change of clothing. Would you drive him to the mall and wait for him while he picks up a few things to carry him over until his baggage arrives?"

"Yes, Mr. James," Glenn answered respectfully, nodding politely at the older man beside his employer. "This way, Mr. Anderson."

Mr. Anderson smiled gratefully at Matt. "I really appreciate this. Everything seems to be going wrong on this business trip."

"We'll do everything we can to make it easier for you," Matt promised, then motioned for Glenn to proceed. When they were gone, he turned back to the desk. "Anything else?" he asked the attractive young woman watching him with shy deference.

"No, sir, Mr. James. Everything's just fine."

"Okay, Vicki. Let me know if anything else comes up. I'll be in my office."

"Yes, Mr. James. Thank you, sir."

Matt swallowed a chuckle as he moved away from the desk. The nineteen-year-old desk clerk had a massive crush on him. He was aware of it and made a special effort to be nice to her without giving any encouragement to her infatuation. It wasn't that uncommon a situation; he was young, knew himself to be attractive enough to the opposite sex and held a position of authority that tended to awe the youngest, most impressionable members of his staff.

He winced at the thought that Melinda would be joining the ranks of his employees on the following

Monday. If only he could expect *her* to show him such awed respect, he thought with rueful whimsy. As the time of his sister's arrival had drawn nearer, he'd been more and more convinced that he'd made a terrible mistake in offering her a summer job. For several reasons. He and Melinda had never gotten along very well, though neither would have denied the strong bonds of familial love between them. Living and working together for ten weeks just might prove more than either of them could survive.

And then there was Brooke. He stared moodily at the walls of his office, thinking—as he did so often—of Brooke.

It had been almost a week since they'd become lovers. During that time Brooke had completely stopped fighting him—about their relationship or anything else, for that matter. She saw him when they could get together, welcomed him eagerly into her arms—and her bed. Their lovemaking was incredible. He'd never experienced anything like it. He couldn't believe that each time kept getting better. And yet . . .

Something wasn't right. It wasn't exactly that he *wanted* Brooke to fight him, but he missed her feisty spirit. He even missed those times when she'd lift her pretty chin and defy him to challenge her. During the past few days she'd gone out of her way not to make waves. Matt sensed that she was still pessimistically waiting for some terrible end to their relationship, but considered herself doing everything in her power to delay it. And he didn't know how to talk to her about it, how to convince her that she was being ridiculous. Dammit, why wouldn't she give them a chance?

It would be even more difficult to further their relationship with Melinda around. Obviously they would have to restrain their lovemaking to Brooke's bed, since Melinda would be sharing Matt's suite. And, though he despised hypocrisy, Matt still felt somewhat uncomfortable with the idea of having his little sister know that he was spending his nights with Brooke.

His eyes focused broodingly on the calendar. Only five more days until Monday. Oh, hell, why had he ever thought having Melinda in Nashville would work out?

BROOKE'S TELEPHONE WAS ringing as she let herself into her apartment on Friday evening. Sighing, she hurried to the phone, already knowing the caller would be Matt. She'd told him she'd be busy that evening, but she hadn't realized how late she would be getting in. "Do you know what time it is?" he demanded the moment she said hello.

"Yes, Matt, I know what time it is," she answered wearily, running a hand through her tangled hair. "The wedding reception ran later than I'd expected, and then we had to take all the decorations down and get them back to the shop. I told you I'd be working late tonight."

"Brooke, I don't like you being out by yourself in the middle of the night."

"It's hardly the middle of the night, Matt. It's only a little past eleven."

"It's eleven-forty," he corrected flatly. "And you've been out alone in that junk heap you call a car."

Hot words of protest sprang to her lips, but she swallowed them with an effort. "There's nothing wrong with my car, Matt."

"Brooke, I drove it yesterday, remember? It barely runs."

He was exaggerating. The car ran a bit rough, yes, but it only needed a tune-up. She'd promised to take care of it as soon as she had the chance. "Matt, I'm sorry you were worried," she said in her most conciliatory tone. "I'm fine, really."

There was a long pause on his end of the line, and then he spoke again, more quietly this time. "I was yelling at you again, wasn't I?"

She grimaced. "Yes, you were."

"I'm sorry."

Her brows shot up in surprise. Matt apologizing? So humbly? She should have been gratified, and yet...something just wasn't right. They just didn't seem to be themselves lately, not since they'd become lovers. How long could they go on hiding their real feelings behind these so careful facades? she wondered bleakly. "It's all right, Matt. Listen, I'm really tired. I think I'll turn in."

"I wish I were there with you. I'll miss having you in my arms tonight."

She swallowed hard at the low-spoken words. "I wish you were here, too," she whispered. Only when they were making love did everything seem perfect between them. Only then did they communicate honestly and unrestrainedly.

"I'll see you tomorrow afternoon, okay?"

"Yes, see you then."

"And, Brooke?"

"Yes, Matt?"

He paused only a moment. "I only worry about you because I love you. You know that, don't you? I couldn't bear it if anything happened to you."

She closed her eyes, her fingers gripping the receiver so tightly they ached. He hadn't told her before—not in words. She was compelled to answer honestly. "I love you, too, Matt."

There was a smile in his voice when he spoke again. "Good night, Brooke. Sleep well."

Murmuring a response, she waited until he'd hung up before replacing her own receiver. Matt loved her, she thought, slumping onto the couch. She loved him. She should be so happy.

And yet she was so very afraid. She buried her face in her hands. Two people could love each other and still hurt each other. She thought of the man she'd loved before. He'd loved her, too, but she'd finally discovered that he'd loved her father's money and power even more. She couldn't live with that.

Love wasn't always enough. Particularly when both people involved were tiptoeing around each other to avoid the quarrels that would have come naturally to them. How long could it be, she wondered, until the tempers they were so ruthlessly subduing exploded into a violent conflagration that would leave their love in ashes?

MATT BARELY GAVE BROOKE time to close her door behind him Saturday afternoon before he had her in his arms, kissing her passionately. She emerged breathless, somewhat bruised, and smiling. "What was that for?" she asked, her arms locked around his neck.

"Tell me again," he demanded, holding her even closer, if that were possible.

She knew what he wanted. "I love you, Matt."

He groaned and kissed her again. "Oh, sweetheart, I've been going crazy wanting to hold you ever since you told me on the phone last night. Wanting to see your face when you said it. Tell me again."

"I love you, Matt," she answered obligingly, laughing at his boyish pleasure in the words. "I love you. I love you. I—"

He swallowed the rest of her words, his mouth taking hers in a consuming, possessive assault. As he kissed her, his right hand slipped beneath her soft pastel-striped sweater, gliding up her back and around to cup one full breast. Brooke arched unconsciously to push herself more firmly into his palm, murmuring her pleasure when his thumb rotated slowly over her hardening nipple.

"I want you, Brooke. I need you."

In answer, she pulled away to take his hand in hers, turning to lead him toward her bedroom.

Stripping rapidly out of his clothing, Matt then undressed her much more slowly, stopping occasionally to explore her body with his hands and his mouth. He dipped his head to lavish kisses on both her swollen, aching breasts, leaving them flushed and damp. Dropping to his knees in front of her, he eased her cotton slacks down her legs, then pressed his face to her stomach, nibbling the skin around her navel. His hands on her hips held her still as he trailed hot, moist kisses down her stomach to the top of her tiny bikini panties. Bracing herself with her hands on his shoulders, Brooke inhaled deeply and closed her eyes, glorying in his caresses. She felt no shyness, no awkwardness as his fingers slipped inside her panties and peeled them down her legs. This was Matt.

He sat back on his heels, sliding his hands upward from her ankles to her thighs, his face a picture of intense concentration. His left hand paused to slip behind her right thigh, steadying her as his right hand trailed inward, his fingertips combing through the tangle of light brown curls between her legs. Brooke drew in a sharp breath as those fingers slipped lower, dipping into the dewy proof of her need for him. He looked up at her, his face blurred by the haze of desire filming her heavy-lidded eyes. "I love you," he said, his voice rough with emotion.

"I love you, t— Oh, *Matt*," she moaned as his mouth replaced his fingers.

And then she cried out again, her words unintelligible this time as her body convulsed violently against him. Her knees lost their stiffening; Matt caught her as she fell forward. He tumbled backward until they both lay sprawled on the carpet, Brooke draped over him. Before she could catch her breath, he gripped her hips in his large, strong hands and arched upward, thrusting deep inside her. Without pausing he began a hard, driving rhythm, his fingers clenching and unclenching in the soft flesh of her buttocks. Still quivering from the pleasure he'd already given her, Brooke found herself unexpectedly responding, desire returning full force. Her movements became as bold, as demanding as his, until the moment when they shuddered together in glorious fulfillment.

Their breathing sounded harshly in the otherwise quiet room as they lay limply tangled, trying to pull themselves together. "I can't understand," Matt murmured after a while, "how it can keep getting better between us. Every time I think it'll never be that good again, and still the next time is even more incredible."

Pleased by his words, and knowing exactly how he felt, Brooke snuggled more deeply into his shoulder. "Matt," she said a few minutes later.

"Mm?"

"We're lying on the floor."

He chuckled, his chest vibrating beneath her. "Yes, we are, aren't we?"

"We have a lovely, comfortable bed right beside us."

"Mm. Think we can find the energy to climb into it?"

"We could try."

"Okay. On three. One. Two." He sprang to his feet, belying his lazy words, and reached down for her. "Three," he said as he brought her to her feet in one smooth tug. Moments later they were cuddled together beneath a pink-flowered sheet.

"You're right. This *is* more comfortable," Matt announced, seemingly surprised by the discovery.

She giggled at his silliness and ran a hand down his smooth, tanned chest. "I thought it might be."

"You're so smart."

"Yes, I know."

"Modest, too."

"Mm. And don't forget incredibly beautiful."

"I could never forget that, sweetheart. It's something I notice every time I look at you."

She blushed at his suddenly serious tone. Of course she'd only been teasing about being incredibly beautiful—she knew full well that she wasn't—but if Matt wanted to agree, she certainly wasn't going to argue with him.

They lay quietly for a time, and then Matt shifted, propping himself on one elbow to smile down at her. "Got any plans for tomorrow?"

"No, I'm free."

"Melinda's plane is supposed to arrive at five-ten. I was hoping you'd go with me to pick her up, then the three of us could go out for dinner. What do you say?"

"Melinda may prefer to have her brother to herself on her first evening in town."

"Are you kidding? She'd be delighted to have someone else along to distract me from her. She thinks if I have nothing better to do, I entertain myself by trying to tell her how to run her life."

Brooke smiled. "And do you?"

"Sometimes," he admitted. "Prerogative of an older brother. Will you go with me to pick her up?"

"If you really want me to."

"I really want you to," he assured her, one finger stroking her cheek. "I hope Melinda doesn't get in the way too often—between us, I mean."

"You'll want to spend some time with her. I understand that."

"I want to spend time with you," he corrected her firmly. "As much time as possible. My sister will have to find some friends of her own age to spend time with—once I've approved them, of course," he added with a wry smile.

"Of course," she agreed, knowing he hadn't been completely joking. Matt's overprotective streak would extend to his family as well as to Brooke, she thought, remembering that phone call the night before. When he cared, he seemed to assume full responsibility for the ones he cared about. Which was sweet, in a way, but could also be very frustrating.

"What about your own family, Brooke?" he asked suddenly, surprising her with the abrupt change of subject. "Have you talked to your parents lately?"

"I talked to my mother last weekend," she replied, becoming somewhat defensive. "I do keep in touch with them, Matt."

"You really should try to patch things up with your father, honey. Family is important."

"I'm aware of that, Matt." Again she had swallowed her protests at his arrogant pronouncement for the sake of peace. How much longer could she continue to do so? "Does Melinda know we've been seeing each other?" she asked to guide the conversation into a less dangerous topic.

He shook his head. "No, I haven't told her. I mentioned to Merry that I've been seeing someone special, but I haven't told her any details yet. I want you to meet them, Brooke. All of them. I want you to go with me when I take Melinda home in August."

He was making plans for them ten weeks in advance. Brooke didn't want to think that far ahead for them yet, but she nodded and told him she'd think about his invitation. Seeing that he wasn't completely satisfied with her answer, she lifted a hand to his cheek. "Kiss me, Matt."

He complied willingly, pulling her close against him as he kissed her slowly, thoroughly. "You're not always going to get away with this," he warned her, his hand already moving to cup one breast.

"What's that?" she asked softly, her own hand stroking his thigh before slipping boldly inward.

"Distracting me with—" He caught his breath, his eyes darkening. "Oh, hell," he muttered, lowering his head to hers. "We'll talk about it later."

9

"HI, MATT! BROOKE!" Melinda squealed, catching sight of the woman at her brother's side. "Hi! It's great to see you." With her natural impulsiveness, she gave Brooke a quick hug. Pleased, Brooke returned the warm embrace.

"I like that," Matt protested in exaggerated indignance. "I get a 'hi, Matt,' and Brooke gets a hug. You've known me for nineteen years, and you met her for fifteen minutes."

Melinda laughed and hugged her brother. "She made a better impression." Standing back, she tossed her heavy strawberry-blond hair out of her strikingly made-up face and looked approvingly from Matt to Brooke. "I knew you were too smart to let this one get away, Matthew."

Brooke felt her cheeks warm immediately. She'd almost forgotten that Melinda tended to say whatever was on her mind.

"Careful, Melinda, that was almost a compliment." Placing himself between the two women, Matt ushered them in the direction of the baggage-claim area. "Let's go see how many pack mules we're going to have to rent to carry your bags."

"I packed light," Melinda retorted. "Merry helped me decide what to bring."

Matt looked at Brooke with a grimace. "That's not necessarily good news. Merry may not have as many clothes as Melinda, but they both carry everything they own even if they'll only be gone for a few hours."

Melinda may not have brought everything she owned, but she'd certainly made an effort. Brooke laughed as Matt piled bag upon bag, scolding the entire time, while Melinda heatedly declared each item she'd brought with her to be utterly necessary.

"Let me help you with those, Mr. James." Glenn, the hotel driver, stepped forward from the curb as soon as Matt appeared with his burden.

"Matt, you brought the limo!" Melinda exclaimed in delight.

"I knew we'd need a big trunk. Melinda, this is Glenn Danvers. Glenn, my sister, Melinda James."

"Nice to meet you, Miss James." The pleasant-featured young man touched a hand to the brim of the dark cap sitting precisely on top of his head.

"Just call me Melinda. We're going to be working together."

"Welcome to the staff, Melinda. Did you want to go straight back to the Amber Rose, Mr. James?"

"Yes. We'll get rid of your bags," he added to Melinda, "then Brooke and I are taking you out to dinner."

"Great. Sounds like fun." Melinda settled into the limousine with a broad, anticipatory smile. "By the way," she asked when Matt and Brooke had taken their places beside her, "does everyone on your staff have to salute when they speak to you?"

Matt's brows drew into a quick frown. "No, they don't have to salute."

"Glenn did everything but click his heels and call you 'your highness,'" Melinda retorted, taking advantage of the closed soundproof divider between the driver and passengers. "I just hope you don't expect that from me."

"All I expect from you is that you remember who's the employer and who's the employee," Matt answered repressively. "You and I won't be seeing each other that often during working hours, anyway. After hours you may continue to behave as obnoxiously as ever."

Ignoring his last sentence, Melinda asked, "Why won't we be seeing each other during working hours?"

"Melinda, you'll be working as a filing clerk in the personnel office. I'll be in my own office most of the time."

"In other words, the boss doesn't mix with the working stiffs."

"I monitor my staff—closely—through the supervisors I have hired for each department. And *you*—"

"How was your flight from Springfield, Melinda?" Brooke asked brightly, sensing an impending quarrel.

Melinda grinned. "Playing peacemaker, Brooke? That's usually my sister Marsha's job."

"And how are your sisters?" Brooke went on, deliberately evading Melinda's question. "Matt told me your oldest sister is expecting a baby."

"Yes, in about six weeks. It's Merry and Grant's second; they've got a really cute little boy, Lucas. Merry's doing fine. I know the whole family would love to meet you, Brooke. I hope you can get to Springfield with Matt soon."

"She's going with us in August when I take you home," Matt put in, taking Brooke's cue to keep the conversation light. Brooke smiled at him in gratitude.

"Hey, that's super! I think you'll like everyone. And I can't wait for you to meet Meaghan, my twin. I'm going to miss her like crazy this summer. It's our first time apart for this long. Merry thinks it'll be good for us and I guess she's right, but I'll still miss her. She— Meaghan, that is—has a new boyfriend. You'd like him, Matt. He's an honor student, president of the student council, conservative dresser. Just your type. Anyway..." She chattered happily during the remainder of the drive to the hotel, hardly pausing for breath as she caught Matt and Brooke up on family news. Probably in deference to Brooke's obvious wish to avoid conflict, Melinda kept her occasional digs at Matt relatively innocuous, and he let them go without retaliation.

MATT ENTERTAINED Brooke and Melinda over dinner with anecdotes from his job in the hotel, making them clutch their sides with laughter as he gave wicked imitations of some of the former guests and their frivolous complaints. "Of course, sometimes their complaints are justified," he added at one point.

"Such as?" Brooke prompted, loving the laughter in his eyes. She had thought there might be some constraint between them with Melinda along, but Melinda's presence actually accomplished just the opposite. Brooke and Matt were able to enjoy being together without all the tension and constraint that so often plagued them when they were alone.

"Well, take last week. A guest—Mr. Anderson—arrived in Nashville only to discover that his luggage had gone to New Guinea or Zambia or some other exotic locale. I had Glenn take him to the closest shopping center so that Mr. Anderson could pick up a few clothes and toiletry items. That evening he had a business dinner with a client, so he put on a new shirt with the suit he was already wearing and left the hotel. While he was gone, one of the maids—a new employee—went in to turn down the bed, didn't see any luggage and decided the guest had checked out. She gathered up the soiled shirt, another shirt and a pair of jeans she found in a drawer, and the toothbrush and shaving gear out of the bathroom, assuming they were left behind by the absentminded guest."

Melinda giggled. "Mr. Anderson really was having rotten luck, wasn't he? His luggage lost and the new items disappearing while he was out to dinner."

Matt nodded, grinning ruefully. "Let's just say he wasn't pleased when he got back to his room. The MOD—manager on duty," he explained for Melinda's benefit, "called me wondering what was going on, and we tracked down the maid and found Mr. Anderson's clothes. We had to replace the toiletry items—she'd thrown those away. Fortunately his luggage arrived the next morning. We saw that it was delivered to his room immediately."

"I hope you weren't too hard on the maid," Melinda commented. "If *I* had done something like that, you'd have had a screaming fit."

"I would not," Matt denied flatly. "And the maid was mildly reprimanded, as she should have been, and won't make such an error again. I am not a slave driver, Melinda."

"So how *was* your flight, Melinda?" Brooke asked hastily when it became apparent that Melinda was going to contest Matt's words. Melinda hesitated for a moment, then laughed and let it go.

After dinner Matt took turns dancing with Brooke and his sister. It wasn't long before Melinda was asked to dance by another man while Matt and Brooke were on the floor. Matt scowled over Brooke's shoulder. "He's old enough to be her father," he complained. "And look how closely he's holding her. Maybe I should—"

"Dance with me and let Melinda take care of herself," Brooke finished for him. "She seems to be enjoying herself. And what could possibly happen right here on the dance floor with you watching their every move?"

"I guess you're right," Matt conceded reluctantly. He risked taking his eyes off his sister for a moment to look down at Brooke. "Are you still going to insist that Melinda and I take you home before we go back to the hotel? I'd rather drop Melinda off at the suite and then take you home alone."

"I think it's best the other way tonight. It *is* her first night in town."

"It's not as if she's never stayed in the suite before," Matt argued, but without much conviction, since he knew Brooke wouldn't change her mind.

"Just for tonight," Brooke promised. "And try not to argue with Melinda when the two of you are alone, will you?"

"She's been starting it," Matt muttered, sounding for all the world like a little boy scolded for fighting with his younger sister.

Brooke had to laugh. "You're the oldest. It's your responsibility to keep the peace," she told him primly.

"*You* should try to live with her for a while," he retorted, though he was smiling again. He dropped a quick kiss on Brooke's uptilted lips. "I want to make love with you," he said gruffly, holding her more snugly against him. "I want to sleep with you in my arms, wake up with you and make love with you again."

Brooke's entire body tightened in response to the sensual images his words evoked. She swallowed a moan, her voice a bit hoarse when she answered. "I want that, too, Matt. We'll work something out while Melinda's here, I promise. It's just...a bit difficult now."

"She's not a child, Brooke. She has to know we're lovers. It's ridiculous to try to hide our relationship from her."

"I'm not trying to hide our relationship from her, Matt. I'm not ashamed that we're lovers. But I don't want to flaunt it in front of your younger sister, either. Nor do you, if you'd be honest," she added meaningfully.

Matt sighed. "I guess you're right. But it's going to be a long ten weeks."

Brooke drew one hand down his chest, rising on her tiptoes to press a soft kiss to his lips. "I don't think you'll have to suffer too greatly during the next ten weeks," she whispered, the words a pledge.

"I love you, Brooke."

"I love you," she returned as the music ended. She turned her head away as they walked back to their table, not wanting Matt to see the sudden, unexpected sheen of tears in her eyes. She didn't know why she felt like crying—except that she was so very much in love with Matt, and still so very much afraid of loving him. By the time they'd rejoined Melinda, Brooke had herself firmly under control.

"SO, HOW ARE THINGS GOING between you and Matt?" Rhonda inquired avidly. Just returned from a two-week vacation, she was eager to catch up on all the details of her employer's unconventional romance.

Brooke sighed and finished misting a hanging basket holding a thriving mixture of *asparagus sprengeri*, *Pteris biaurita*, *Peperomia glabella* and *Ficus pumila*. Only after turning away from the basket did she give her friend a wry smile and make an attempt to answer the question. "About the same," she said. "He's being very careful not to be overly dictatorial, and I'm staying constantly on the defensive in case he slips up. We see each other whenever we can, but Melinda's presence is making things a little complicated since Matt wants to serve as a good example for his impressionable younger sister—as well as keeping an eye on her at all times. He and Melinda have been living and working together for two weeks now, and already they've had about six minor skirmishes and one all-out battle. I'm trying to keep them from each other's throats even as I do the same for Matt and me."

"Oh, brother," Rhonda murmured sympathetically.

"You can say that again. I'm exhausted," Brooke admitted. "Sometimes I feel like admitting defeat and heading for the hills—figuratively speaking."

"And why don't you?" Rhonda asked, though the knowing look in her eyes indicated she already knew the answer.

Brooke grimaced. "Because I'm so crazy in love with Matt James that I can hardly think straight, that's why. Just about the time I decide I can't possibly take any more, Matt shows up on my doorstep for three or four hours of blissfully uninterrupted time together and . . . well, I change my mind."

"Oh, honey, you do have it bad, don't you?"

Brooke ran a hand through her hair and nodded. "Yeah. I've got it bad, dammit."

"And you're still walking around just waiting for the ax to fall," Rhonda observed in audible disgust. "Honestly, Brooke."

"I can't help it, Rhonda," Brooke argued, fighting down a surge of guilt at the accusation. "Matt and I are both working so hard to hold on to what we have. It's not natural. We shouldn't have to change for each other."

"That's ridiculous. No one ever said it was easy to keep a relationship going. Whether it's a love affair or a marriage, it still takes a lot of hard work on both sides to make it last. You're talking to someone with years of experience, remember? You think Bud and I don't ever have rough times? That we don't both have to compromise at times for the sake of the marriage?"

"I know you—"

"Your problem, Brooke Matheny, is that you're a defeatist when it comes to personal relationships."

"I'm not a defeatist!"

"Oh, yeah? So how come you don't go home and see your father, huh? I mean, really sit down and talk to him, settle all your differences?"

"Rhonda, it wouldn't do any good. He and I just can't see eye to eye."

"See what I mean? A defeatist."

Brooke was still arguing when Rhonda left her to wait on a customer. Something told Brooke that Rhonda had made up her mind and wouldn't be swayed by any amount of argument. Rhonda was wrong, of course, Brooke told herself emphatically. Brooke wasn't a defeatist. She was simply a realist. And they were two very different things, she thought with self-righteous conviction.

"IT JUST MAKES ME SICK, Brooke. The people around the Amber Rose treat Matt as if he were God. They do everything but genuflect as he walks by."

Repressing a grin at Melinda's complaint, Brooke took a bite of her hot fudge sundae before responding. She and Melinda had been shopping on this Saturday afternoon following Melinda's third full week on her job at the Amber Rose, and the experience had been a most entertaining one for Brooke. "You have to realize, Melinda, that Matt is their boss. They owe him their respect."

"Their respect, yes, but not blind obedience! It undermines their individual dignities for them to suppress their own opinions and personalities in his presence."

Psychology majors, Brooke thought with a mental shake of her head. She remembered a few from her own college days. "What I hear you saying," she began in a bit of retained psych-ese, "is that you see Matt as no more than a bossy older brother, so you think other people should see him in the same way, is that it?"

Melinda looked startled by the unexpected analysis. "Well, no, I—" She stopped, frowned and toyed with her double-chocolate banana supreme split. "Well, maybe," she admitted at last. "I just don't see anything all that impressive about him."

Brooke laughed. "That's because you've known him for so long. You've seen him with his pants down, so to speak, and you know his flaws and weaknesses. To your co-workers, he's a man who has risen to a position of authority at a very young age, a man who demands perfection from his staff because his job is very important to him, a man who—and this is the clincher—a man who signs their paychecks."

Melinda tilted her head, thought about Brooke's words for a moment, then giggled. "As a matter of fact, I *have* seen him in his underwear. He wasn't particularly modest as a teenager."

Brooke smiled in response. "See? You view Matt from a totally different perspective. That's one of the reasons it's so hard for family members to work together, particularly when one is the other's supervisor."

"I know a few women at work who'd *like* to see Matt with his pants down," Melinda mused wickedly, watching Brooke through her lush lashes for a reaction. "In fact, Vicki, who works on the front desk, would probably give her left arm for the opportunity."

"Tell her to keep both arms on her own body," Brooke suggested sweetly, obligingly going along with Melinda's teasing. "Or I'll gladly remove one of them for her."

Melinda laughed her delight with Brooke's response. "Gosh, I like you, Brooke. I'm glad you and Matt are together. I've never seen him so nutty about anyone, even Susie Carpenter."

"Susie Carpenter?" Brooke repeated politely.

"Yeah. His first serious relationship. He was seventeen. He used to bring her over to our house for dinner sometimes, and afterward they'd go outside in the dark and make out on the front porch swing. Meaghan and I were six, and we'd sneak around from the backyard and make fun of them. Matt threatened to kill us more than once."

Brooke laughed. "I'm sure he did."

"He'd chase us around the house and we'd scream for Mom, who'd always fuss at Matt for frightening his little sisters," Melinda added with relish. "We got a real kick out of it. He finally got wise and quit bringing his girlfriends home with him."

Brooke shook her head. "You and Meaghan were obviously little monsters."

"Well, Meaghan usually just went along with whatever I suggested. I was the one with all the great ideas."

"Now why doesn't that surprise me?"

"I really miss her," Melinda murmured wistfully, then brightened almost immediately. "Tell me, Brooke, are you and Matt going to get married?"

Brooke choked on a bite of ice cream. Hastily swallowing it, she wiped her mouth on a napkin, carefully framing her answer. "We haven't discussed marriage."

"How come. You're in love, aren't you?"

"Melinda, we've only been dating for a relatively short time. It's much too soon to discuss anything as permanent as marriage."

Melinda looked bewildered, as well as exasperated. "What's to discuss? You love each other, so you should get married."

Brooke wondered if she'd ever been so young and so naive, then immediately thought of her former love affair. She *had* been just that naive, assuming Blake had to love her just because she loved him. Assuming that marriage automatically accompanied romance, that true love could overcome any obstacles. That was before she'd become a levelheaded realist, of course.

"If you're finished with your ice cream, we'd better get going," she told Melinda, changing the subject. "We've already been longer than I'd expected, and I still have to get ready for my date with Matt."

Diverted by Brooke's words, Melinda gathered her many packages. "I wish I could see Matt's face when he sees you in that new dress you bought. It's so gorgeous. He'll flip."

He'd more likely rip it off her, Brooke thought with a smug, secret smile, keeping the thought to herself. It had been several days since she and Matt had found the time to be together, and the dress was nothing short of pure seduction.

Something told her it would be very late before she and Matt had dinner that evening.

LESS THAN THREE HOURS LATER, Matt took one look at the sleek blue dress, expertly cut to show the maximum legally and morally acceptable amount of Brooke's creamy skin, and his eyes glazed. "Oh, lady, what you do for silk," he murmured, just before his mouth covered hers.

Brooke had been right. They didn't eat until very late.

"I really was going to take you someplace special tonight," Matt said sheepishly as he finished the omelet Brooke had served him at her cosy dinette table. He wore only the pants to the impeccably tailored blue suit in which he'd arrived, his formerly immaculately brushed hair was rumpled boyishly around his face and his expression was that of a thoroughly satiated male.

Facing him from across the table, her own sexy dress replaced by a lightweight robe, Brooke smiled. "You did take me someplace very special."

His eyes sparkled at the intimate innuendo in her words. "I love you. Have I told you lately?"

"Not in the last five minutes."

"That long? Then I owe you another one. I love you, Brooke."

"I love you, Matt."

"I don't want to go back to the hotel."

"You're welcome to stay here."

He looked tempted, then sighed and shook his head regretfully. "I guess I'd better go. I realize it's silly, but I just don't like the thought of Melinda knowing I've spent the night in your bed."

"It's not silly, Matt. It's just what I'd expect from an overprotective older brother."

He looked at her suspiciously. "Are you making fun of me?"

"Would I do that?" she asked innocently.

"Yes. You would."

Brooke only laughed. "I hope Melinda had a good time tonight with Lynette and Sherry." Smitty's teenage daughters had invited Melinda to accompany them to a concert that evening, an invitation Melinda had eagerly accepted.

"That's another reason I have to go. I want to make sure Melinda got home all right. I'm glad the three of them hit it off so well. Lynette and Sherry are nice girls. If they weren't, Smitty would lock them in their rooms."

Brooke grinned and reached for her coffee cup. "Just what you'd do if you had daughters."

"Exactly," he agreed without a hint of apology. "I'm quite sure I'll be as overprotective a father as I am a big brother. You'll just have to make sure I don't go overboard with it, I suppose."

Brooke swallowed too big a gulp of coffee and spent the next three minutes coughing. Matt pounded enthusiastically on her back until she begged him to stop helping her. As soon as she could speak coherently, she deliberately changed the subject. Matt's eyes danced with laughter at the blatant retreat, but he said no more on the subject of parenthood, for which Brooke was fervently grateful.

He left her reluctantly, with long, lingering kisses and murmured words of love. And an autocratic command to bolt her door the moment he stepped outside. Brooke obeyed, then wandered through the apartment, thinking how suddenly empty it seemed. Matt had been gone for ten minutes and already she missed him desperately, she realized soberly. Crawling into bed, she lay staring at the dark ceiling, thinking of his implication that he and Brooke would someday share the responsibility of child rearing. It wasn't hard to figure out that Matt was thinking of making their relationship permanent and legal.

For just a moment she allowed herself to drift along in a lovely daydream of marriage and babies. And for the first time she allowed herself to admit how very badly she wanted to marry Matt James. How she'd love to have their children.

For the past few years Brooke had taken great pride in being a realist. Until now she hadn't understood that her so-called realism had masked a wide streak of cowardice. Blake had hurt her with his greedy infatuation with her father's money. Her father had hurt her with his airy disregard for her needs and desires. But Matt held the power to hurt her as she'd never been hurt before.

What if it didn't work out? What if something went wrong? What if he changed his mind about loving her? If he demanded more than she could give, as her father had?

Finding no answers to those questions on the bedroom ceiling, she groaned and rolled to her feet. She was tired, but too wound up to sleep. She decided to find a boring movie on the television and do needlework until her eyes crossed, hoping that by then she'd be so exhausted she'd sleep without worrying about her future—or lack of a future—with Matt.

10

"I STILL CAN'T BELIEVE you fired her! Have you no compassion at all?"

Matt faced his sister across the living room of the suite, exasperated with their top-of-the-voice argument, which had been raging for the past fifteen minutes. "Melinda, I'm not going to continue to defend my actions to you. I make the decisions when it comes to the operation of the Amber Rose, and I answer for those decisions only to the owners—not to anyone else, including you!"

A knock on the door caught his attention. "That's Brooke. I don't want to hear any more about this tonight. Is that clear?"

"Yes, it's clear, oh, mighty despot. Your word is law around here." Melinda dropped onto the couch in a sullen slump, her arms crossed over the front of the pink, orange and purple swirled knit dress she'd put on for dinner with her brother and Brooke on this Friday evening at the end of her fourth week in Nashville.

Throwing up his hands in frustration at his sister's behavior, Matt crossed rapidly to the door. Brooke's wary expression indicated that the raised voices had carried into the hallway. He grimaced ruefully at her before leaning over to kiss her. "Hi, sweetheart. You look beautiful."

And she did look beautiful, her thick golden curls piled into a loose knot, her slender body wrapped in a pastel print surplice dress, her brown eyes gazing up at him with sympathetic understanding. Matt wished desperately that they were alone, that he could catch her up in his arms, carry her into the bedroom and make love to her until all his problems had faded into blissful oblivion. It was getting harder all the time to leave her at night, to wait as patiently as possible for the all-too-rare moments when they could be alone. He wanted her with him all the time, wanted her in his bed every night, in his arms every morning when he woke.

"Problems?" she murmured, glancing from him to Melinda's pouting position on the couch.

He lifted one shoulder in a weary shrug. "Aren't there always?"

"What's wrong?"

Matt shook his head. "I'd rather not talk about it right now."

"No, he doesn't want to talk about it," Melinda put in angrily, overhearing the words. "He ruins a young woman's life, takes away her only means of support, and he doesn't want to talk about it. He'd rather just completely put her out of his mind. He doesn't care what will happen to her as long as she's not interfering with the smooth operation of his precious Amber Rose."

"Dammit, Melinda!" Matt exploded, furious at being put into the position of having to justify an action that he hadn't found all that pleasant to begin with. "The woman was stealing from my guests! And that's not the first time I've had trouble with her. She was continually late, often didn't show up for work at all, brought her troubles to work with her and took her anger out on her co-workers or guests of the hotel. I've warned her, I've tried to work with her because I knew she had problems, but I cannot have someone on my staff who steals from the guests, any more than Merry and Marsha could keep someone on staff who'd rob guests at the parties they organize."

"Matt, she's really a nice person inside. It's just that creep she lives with—he spends all the money she makes on booze, then gets drunk and beats her up."

"I'm sorry her life is in such a mess, I really am. She needs a counselor to help her understand why she can't pull herself out of that destructive relationship. But she's also got an attitude problem, Melinda. I tried to talk to her, and she basically told me to go to hell. There was nothing I could do but let her go. At least I didn't prosecute. I could have, you know. She cost the Amber Rose the money to reimburse the guests, not to mention the stain on our reputation."

"Melinda," Brooke said, keeping her voice as soothing as possible, "every employer occasionally has to let an unsatisfactory employee go. I've had to myself, with people who wouldn't pull their weight or who were unpleasant to customers. It's never a pleasant task, but it's sometimes unavoidable."

Matt gave her a grateful smile. Melinda sighed and shrugged. "I'm just worried about what will happen to her now."

"Maybe this incident will force her to look at her life and make the decision to change it," Brooke suggested. "It's nice of you to care about her, Melinda, and I think you'll be a wonderful psychologist someday, but you'll learn then that not everyone will allow themselves to be helped. They have to want to change before anyone can help them."

"Look, why don't we go down and get something to eat," Matt offered, trying to make peace.

"That sounds like a wonderful idea," Brooke agreed brightly. "I'm starving."

Matt caught her hand in his and squeezed it gently, thanking heaven she was there. Melinda squirmed on the couch, then looked up half defiantly at Matt. "Lynette and Sherry asked me to come over and watch movies on their VCR with them tonight. I think I'll go on now."

"Melinda, we'd planned to have dinner together," Matt argued.

Brooke's fingers tightened in Matt's. Taking the hint, he exhaled and nodded. "Okay, fine. If you want to go over to Smitty's, go ahead. Just don't stay out too late, okay? I don't like you out by yourself after midnight."

Melinda rolled her eyes but refrained from comment.

"You need cab fare?"

"I have money."

"Fine. Brooke and I are going down to eat. See you later."

Her hand still clasped in Matt's, Brooke looked back at Melinda. "Maybe you and I can do something together tomorrow afternoon. There's a big sidewalk sale at the mall."

"Yeah, maybe."

"I'll call you in the morning."

"All right. See you, Brooke."

Brooke waited until she and Matt were in the elevator before speaking again. "She means well, Matt."

Matt lifted a hand to his neck and wearily massaged the knotted muscles there. "I know. She just has a lot of growing up to do. She's pretty immature for nineteen."

"No more than I was."

He pulled her into his arms for a hug, suddenly needing that more than anything else he could imagine. "I wish I'd known you when you were nineteen. I'll bet you were a cute teenager."

She rubbed her cheek on his shoulder and laughed softly. "I'm afraid I was a lot like Melinda. Idealistic, rebellious, naive."

"And when did you get to be so mature and realistic?" he teased, smiling down at her.

Her own smile faded abruptly, making Matt wonder what he'd said to sadden her. "Three years ago," she answered quietly, pulling out of his arms as the elevator bumped lightly to a stop on the ground floor.

Three years ago. The year she'd broken away from her family and set out to find herself in Nashville. Not long after the end of the romance Matt had found out about only after relentless questioning. Even then she'd been frustratingly reticent about both events in her life. He walked thoughtfully beside her to the restaurant, wishing he knew more about the men who'd made her so afraid to relinquish even the smallest amount of control over her life—her father and her former lover. He hated the thought of Brooke loving another man. He intended to make sure that there was never another man but him in her life. Ever.

THEY HAD BARELY BEEN SEATED at Matt's reserved table when he was confronted quite unexpectedly by

Brooke's past. He'd noticed the older, distinguished-looking man who'd watched from a nearby table as Matt and Brooke had been escorted across the room by the solicitous maître d'. The man waited only until they were seated before rising from his own table to cross the room to them. With barely a glance at Matt the man looked at Brooke. "Hello, Brooke."

Brooke looked up curiously from her menu, then gasped. "Dad! What are you doing here?"

"I'm staying here. Checked in this afternoon," Nathan Matheny answered impassively. He turned to look at Matt, who'd risen to his feet at Brooke's identification of the older man. "And this is—?"

"Matt James," Matt supplied, offering his hand as he closely studied the other man. He saw little of Brooke in the sharply carved, sternly set features. She must look like her mother, he decided, even as he added, "I'm the manager of the Amber Rose."

Matheny nodded, though Matt wondered at the expression in his piercingly sharp gray eyes. It was as if Brooke's father hadn't been at all surprised to hear Matt's name, nor surprised to find his daughter dining in the very hotel where he was staying in Nashville. Had Matheny somehow found out about Brooke's relationship with Matt? "Just call me Nathan," the older man said, and the words came out more as an order than a friendly suggestion. "I guess you've figured out that I'm Brooke's father."

"Yes. Have you eaten, Nathan?"

"No, not yet."

"Then won't you please join us?" Matt indicated the third place setting at the table. "My sister was going to dine with us, but she's gone out with friends."

Nathan glanced at his daughter, who was sitting very still in her own seat, her face rather pale. "Brooke?"

"Yes, Dad. Please join us," she said quietly.

Nodding again in the curt gesture that seemed characteristic of the man, Nathan settled into the extra chair. "How have you been, Brooke?"

"I'm fine, thank you. What are you doing in Nashville?" Brooke asked again.

Deciding she still looked shaken by her father's unexpected appearance, Matt discreetly took her hand beneath the table, not surprised to find her fingers icy. He squeezed reassuringly and she clung fiercely to his hand, almost cutting off his circulation. Was she that intimidated by her father? Matt wondered, his eyes narrowing.

"I came to see you, Brooke. It was becoming quite apparent that you had no immediate plans to come home for a visit with your mother and me. Is it so strange that I'd want to know how my daughter was doing after three years?"

"I call at least once a month to let you know that I'm well," Brooke replied, her voice defensive.

"A telephone call is not the same as seeing for myself," Nathan returned implacably.

The waiter arrived then to take the orders, drawing Nathan's attention away from his daughter. But not for long. The moment the orders had been placed, Nathan began to question Brooke—about her health, her business, her life in Nashville. Not so subtly criticizing the decisions she'd made in the past three years. The arrival of their meal did not stop the flow of questions. Matt tried to defend Brooke by pointing out how successful Ribbons & Blossoms had become, but that only led to Nathan asking why Brooke hadn't already opened another shop.

"I intend to, Dad, when the timing is right," she answered quietly.

"I'll come by and look over your operation in the morning. Perhaps I'll have some suggestions," Nathan informed her.

And then he turned to Matt, as Matt had been expecting him to do for some time. "What about you, young man? How long have you been seeing my daughter?"

"Dad—"

Matt placed a hand on Brooke's knee. "Brooke and I have been seeing each other for a couple of months, Nathan. She's very special to me."

Nathan's steel-gray eyes cut sharply from Matt to Brooke. "Serious, is it?"

"Yes, sir. Very serious," Matt returned evenly, when Brooke seemed about to protest her father's personal questions.

"You plan to run this hotel for the rest of your life?"

"Matt wants to eventually own his own vacation resort in the Nashville area," Brooke cut in, seeming to have taken offense at the tone of her father's question. "He and a partner have already completed most of the preliminary planning."

"Is that right?" Interested, as always, in anything concerning business, Nathan turned fully toward Matt. "Tell me about it. I've been known to invest in such ventures on occasion."

"If you'll excuse me," Brooke said, dropping her napkin on the table, "I need to freshen up."

Matt watched her walk away, her back stiff, chin high, and resisted the impulse to go after her and take her in his arms. He made no effort to hide his anger when he looked at her father. "If this is the way you always treat her, it's no wonder she's avoided seeing you for three years."

"I need no advice about the way to talk to my daughter, young man," Nathan answered quietly.

"Obviously you do."

It was just as obvious that Nathan Matheny was not accustomed to having his word disputed. His gray eyebrows shot up, though Matt thought there was a gleam of respect in the other man's eyes. "From what I've heard," Nathan remarked, "you're a man who doesn't mince words any more than I do. You run your staff here with a firm hand, allowing no nonsense. A man much like myself, in fact. Which is one reason I decided to come meet you in person. I would have thought Brooke would have nothing to do with anyone who reminded her of me."

Matt leaned back in his chair, not at all surprised by Nathan's revelation. "That did concern her at the beginning. Now I understand why. You've had her watched, haven't you?"

"I know everything my daughter has done for the past three years," Nathan admitted blandly. "I know exactly how much money her business earns, who her most frequent customers are, the names and addresses of her friends and the names of each of the other men she has dated in Nashville. Before you she was seeing a young doctor; there was some speculation that the two of them would be married."

"You should never listen to speculation."

"I rarely do."

"I suppose you also know quite a bit about me?"

"Matthew Lucas James, age thirty. You have a degree in hotel management from a university in Missouri, close to your hometown of Springfield, Missouri. Your parents are dead; you have four sisters, three of whom are still living in Springfield, two married to partners in a successful computer consulting firm. Your other sister is currently living with you and working in the hotel. Your annual income is in the mid-five-figure range, and the man with whom you plan to go into business is an accountant by the name of Ken Lincoln.

"Though you are popular with women, you have an excellent reputation and are known for treating the women you date with respect and consideration. Prior to your sister's arrival in Nashville, you spent many of your nights in my daughter's apartment, as she did in yours. The doctor who preceded you in her affections never spent the night with her. Did I leave anything out?"

"Just one thing," Matt replied with ruthlessly maintained control. "Your daughter is an intelligent, level-headed, hardworking businesswoman who has earned her success with no help from you or anyone else. Any man who doesn't respect her for that is an utter fool."

"I am no fool, Matthew. I have a great deal of respect for my daughter. She had a brilliant future ahead of her in my corporation."

"A future you planned for her. A future controlled by you. She is quite capable of arranging her own life."

"I'll admit that she has accomplished more than I'd expected when she took off in such a rage three years ago. And I am pleased that she has chosen a man with spirit and brains such as you. My wife and I want our daughter back in our lives, Matthew. I can make it worth your while to help us get her there. Let's talk more about this resort idea of yours."

BY THE TIME Brooke's father boarded his plane for Denver on Saturday afternoon, she was exhausted. He had spent the entire morning in her shop, going over her books and her method of operation. She wasn't sure exactly why she'd allowed his inspection of her business; perhaps she'd only wanted to prove to him that she was quite capable of making a success of herself without his help. If she'd expected any words of praise from him, she was destined to be disappointed.

Rather to her surprise, Nathan said little about Matt other than to remark that he "had a head on his shoulders" and "wasn't a spineless parasite like that other one"—this in reference to Brooke's disastrous affair with Blake. She wasn't surprised that Nathan approved of Matt. After all, she'd watched them sitting side by side at dinner and she'd seen two kindred souls.

She suspected that Nathan would invest in Matt's resort. He'd asked endless questions about Matt's plans on the previous evening, questions Matt had answered with careful politeness, if little emotion. Would Matt be even more determined to possess her now that he realized the package included a wealthy, influential father-in-law? she wondered wearily.

Her telephone rang soon after she returned from the airport. As she'd suspected, it was Matt.

"Is he gone?"

"He's gone," Brooke answered listlessly, dragging one hand through her hair.

"I'm on my way over."

"No! Matt, please."

There was a long pause on Matt's end of the line. "You don't want me to come over?"

She closed her eyes and tried to keep her voice calm. "Matt, I'm so tired. I feel as if I've been through an inquisition. I really need some time alone. Please."

"All right, Brooke, if that's what you want," he answered quietly, and she knew she'd hurt him. Her eyes filled with tears that she forced back until after she'd concluded the call. "I just thought you might need someone to talk to," he added.

"Matt . . . I'll talk to you tomorrow, all right?"

"All right. Get some rest, sweetheart. I love you."

"I—" Her voice caught in a sob she'd been unable to restrain. "I'll talk to you tomorrow, Matt."

The tears came after she'd hung up the phone. Matt had wanted to come to her to cheer her up after her father's visit. He'd thought she was upset by her father's constant criticism and endless questioning. She was upset by that, of course. But she was more upset over her relationship with Matt. Those hours spent with Nathan had brought back all the fears she'd been trying to ignore for the past few weeks, all the questions about whether she wanted to spend her life with a man so accustomed to being in control.

Marriage to Matt would not be the modern, practical, businesslike arrangement she'd envisioned with Gary, she thought soberly. Matt would not be content to allow her to go her own way, make her own plans, maintain her own separate identity. He'd want to know where she was going, when she'd be home, who she was seeing—just as he did with Melinda. And when it came down to a split decision, she had no doubt that Matt would consider his word final. He had been in a position of authority too long to give up that power without resistance.

She'd spent less than twenty-four hours with her father, and she felt as if she'd been pulled backward through a keyhole. Drained, exhausted just from fighting to have her own opinions recognized. She'd left Denver simply because she couldn't live that way any longer. Wouldn't she be making a terrible mistake to willingly step back into such a situation? To give up her hard-won freedom to Matt?

There would be passion in a marriage to Matt. Passion and love. But could those ephemeral emotions survive the harsh realities of daily living?

By the time her tears had dried, she was no closer to an answer. She only knew that she loved Matt with all her heart, and having to choose between that love and her own precious independence was tearing her apart.

MATT DIDN'T BOTHER to call before showing up Sunday afternoon; perhaps he'd been afraid that she'd ask him to stay away again. "Where's Melinda?" Brooke asked after she'd let him in.

"Spending the day at the lake with Lynette and Sherry. I have a feeling the three of them are cruising for guys today."

"They're normal teenagers; that's probably exactly what they're doing. Would you like something to drink?"

"No." He caught her forearms in his hands, forcing her to look up at him. "How are you?"

"I'm fine, Matt. Really," she assured him.

"All over your father's visit?"

She grimaced, trying to treat the subject with humor. "I survived."

He shook his head slowly. "You weren't exaggerating about him, were you? He's tough as nails."

"That's my dad." She pulled away from him. "I think I'll have a glass of iced tea. Are you sure you don't want something, Matt?"

"Yes, I want something. I want you," he answered impatiently. "What's wrong, Brooke?"

"Wrong? Nothing's wrong. Why do you ask?"

"Sweetheart, I know you. Something's bothering you, and I'm not so sure it's just your father. Now what is it?"

"Really, Matt, it's nothing," she lied, blandly meeting his eyes. "Everything's fine."

He didn't look at all satisfied with her answer. Seeing that he wasn't going to let it go, she allowed herself to do what she'd been wanting to do since she'd opened the door to find him there. Stepping close to him, she rose on her tiptoes to press her mouth to his. "I missed you yesterday," she told him, and this time she wasn't lying. She had missed him desperately during the night, so much so that she'd awakened reaching for him and then had to fight back tears when he hadn't been there.

"You're doing it again, aren't you?" he scolded, taking her in his arms.

"Feel free to stop me at any time," she offered mischievously, trailing one finger down the front of his close-fitting knit shirt.

He groaned and lowered his forehead to hers. "You're overestimating my willpower. You know I have no resistance to you at all."

"Good," she whispered. "I like knowing I'm not totally defenseless against you."

He cupped her face between his hands, frowning down at her. "What was that supposed to mean?"

"It means that I want to make love with you," she evaded skillfully, covering his hands with hers. "Now."

"Brooke, I—" He stopped abruptly when her hand slipped between them. "Let's go to the bedroom."

They made love slowly at first, savoring each moment as though it were the first time, and then desperately, as though it would be the last time. Matt explored every inch of Brooke's body, tasting, teasing, nibbling until she writhed helplessly beneath him, hot flames licking down her spine to meet at the junction of her thighs. When she could stand no more, she pushed against him, rolling him onto his back so that she could return the favor. Matt stood as many of her fevered caresses as he could, and then he ground out a sound that was somewhere between curse and endearment and settled forcefully between her thighs.

Her hands clenched at his shoulders, her legs locked around his lean, driving hips, Brooke arched upward, her eyes closed, willingly blocking out everything but Matt's lovemaking.

"I love you, Brooke. God, how I love you," he muttered into her throat.

"I love you, Matt," she whispered, just before she was swept away on a shattering wave of pleasure. "Oh, Matt!"

Some time later, his breathing still ragged, Matt cradled Brooke against his shoulder and stroked her damp hair. "Better every time," he murmured.

She smiled and snuggled deeper. "Yes."

"I love you."

"I love you, too, Matt."

Matt shifted suddenly until she was lying on her back with him leaning over her. His eyes grave, he cupped her cheek with one hand. Brooke swallowed hard, guessing what was coming. She was right.

"Marry me, Brooke."

11

BROOKE PUSHED HER HAIR out of her face and reached for her robe, which was draped across the foot of the bed. Avoiding Matt's eyes, but aware that he had gone very still, she stood and belted herself into the thigh-length robe. "I think I'll make some coffee."

"I'd like an answer, Brooke."

"Yes, I know. I...I really need some coffee," she blurted out, then turned and hurried out of the room.

Matt stared at the doorway for several minutes, then slammed one clenched fist down on the bed. Damn! She was running from him again. It had been too soon to propose. She wasn't ready, wasn't over the trauma of her father's visit. During the past couple of weeks he had made great progress in getting her to trust him, to recognize and acknowledge the love between them. Now, it seemed, he was back to square one.

Why couldn't he have waited, given her more time? he asked himself with a mental groan, climbing out of the bed and stepping into his jeans. But he knew why. He wanted her for his wife. Wanted that now. He was tired of living apart from her.

He wouldn't lose her. She needed time; fine. He'd give her time. But not too much. He wouldn't be able to last much longer.

Brooke was bustling busily around the kitchen when he joined her. She sensed his presence without looking up. "Want a cup of coffee, Matt? How about a slice of cake? It's fresh carrot cake."

"Just coffee, thanks." He stepped up behind her and dropped his hands on her shoulders, regretting the way she immediately stiffened at his touch. "It's all right, Brooke. You don't have to answer me today."

"I . . . don't?"

"No. It seems obvious enough that you weren't ready for me to ask."

"No. No, I wasn't."

Very gently he turned her around to face him. "I love you, Brooke. I've never loved another woman as deeply as I love you. In my experience people who love each other eventually want to marry and start a family together. I want what my parents had, what my married sisters have, but I can wait until you're ready. Until you've worked through whatever fears you have about our relationship."

"Oh, Matt." Brooke raised a hand to his cheek, her huge brown eyes shining with unshed tears. "I wish I could say yes. I . . . I want to say yes. But, as you said, there are things I have to work out first. Just . . . just give me time, okay?"

"All the time you need, sweetheart," he promised huskily, hoping he'd have the patience to stand by that vow.

"I really do love you, Matt."

"I know." He kissed her lightly, then stepped back from her. "Maybe I will have some of that cake. Fresh carrot cake, you said?"

"Mm. I made it myself."

"Make it a big piece, then."

The smile she gave him was tremulous, grateful. "Pour yourself a cup of coffee. I'll cut the cake."

"This is delicious," Matt said enthusiastically a few minutes later. "If I'd known you could bake like this, I'd have proposed even sooner."

Brooke surprised herself by laughing at his quip. She could have hugged him for easing the tension remaining from his proposal with teasing and light conversation. She was actually surprised that he'd allowed her to get away with her evasion of the issue. She would have expected him to demand an immediate reply to his proposal. Maybe, she thought with cautious optimism, maybe he *would* be able to convince her in time that their relationship—maybe even marriage—would work for them. She found herself praying that he could.

"Tell me about your mother, Brooke. What's she like?" Matt asked unexpectedly.

She tilted her head in curiosity at the question. "My mother? Why do you ask?"

He shrugged and sipped his coffee. Setting the cup on the table, he picked up his fork again. "Just curious. Now that I've met your father, I'd like to know about your mother. You haven't said much about her."

Brooke considered her answer carefully. "My mother is very sweet, very soft-spoken. She's perfectly happy taking care of her home and her flower garden, meeting with her bridge club and volunteering at the local hospital. She and I aren't very much alike, though people often remark at how closely I resemble her in appearance."

"Does she and your father get along?"

"Oh, sure. He tells her what to do, and she does it. It works for both of them." She tried not to let resentment color her voice, though she'd always resented her mother's quiet acceptance of her husband's authority. It would have been nice if Olivia had occasionally backed Brooke up when she'd rebelled.

"It wouldn't be like that for us," Matt said meaningfully, making Brooke realize that she hadn't been entirely successful at hiding her feelings.

No, it wouldn't be that way for her and Matt, she thought grimly. She'd never be able to meekly follow orders as her mother had done for the past thirty-odd years. Brooke would resist every effort to dominate her, and would lose her fiery temper, resulting in heated quarrels.

How long would it be before Matt grew tired of the battles, found himself looking for a woman more like Brooke's mother, a woman who was perfectly happy following orders?

"I'm really looking forward to the big fireworks display at Opryland Tuesday night," Brooke commented, blatantly changing the subject. "I adore fireworks. It wouldn't be the Fourth of July without them, would it?"

Matt followed her conversational lead, but the look he gave her told her that he wouldn't allow her to get away with her evasions forever. She didn't expect him to. She was going to have to make some major decisions. Soon. If only she knew what those decisions should be.

MATT STAYED VERY BUSY during the holiday week that followed his proposal to Brooke. He didn't mention marriage again, but she knew he was waiting with strained patience for her to give him an answer. Matt was not a naturally patient man. When he wanted something, he wanted it immediately. And he wanted Brooke.

Melinda wasn't making things easier for them. Growing restless with her routine paperwork job in the personnel department, she began to interfere in other areas of the hotel management. Once she'd almost made the chef quit by accusing him of using too much salt in his cooking, then lecturing him on modern theories of health and nutrition. Matt had had to do some fast talking to soothe the man's ruffled sensibilities. Later, of course, he'd had some choice words for Melinda.

Aware of Matt's growing tension, Brooke continued to expect an explosion, to Rhonda's disgust. After forcing Brooke to admit that Matt had proposed, Rhonda couldn't understand how Brooke could claim to love Matt and still be unwilling to commit herself to him. To Rhonda, it was simple. One fell in love, one married and had children. It had worked for her and her Bud; why not for Brooke and Matt?

On Friday morning Brooke was delighted to receive a telephone call from Gary. It had been over two weeks since she'd talked to him, and she'd missed spending time with him, missed his unthreatening friendship, his continuous teasing, his never-fail ability to make her smile.

"Gary!" she said in undisguised pleasure. "It's good to hear your voice."

Gary laughed at the enthusiasm of her greeting. "I thought I'd give you a call and see how things are going. Sounds like it's a good thing I did."

"My father showed up last weekend."

"Uh-oh. Was it bad?" her friend asked sympatheti- cally, knowing the full story of Brooke's break with her parent.

"Awful. He did everything but check my teeth."

"Poor kid. Did he also check out Matt?"

"Yes. One businessman to another. I think he ap- proved."

"You don't sound all that happy about it."

"Gary, my father *approved* of Matt," Brooke re- peated meaningfully.

"Ah," Gary murmured in understanding. "You don't necessarily want to be involved with a man your fa- ther approves of, right?"

"You got it." Brooke's fingers tightened on the re- ceiver as a sudden thought occurred to her. "Gary, are you doing anything for lunch?"

"No, why?"

"Let's get together, okay? We could meet somewhere close to the hospital."

"I'd love to, honey, but I'm not going to get my face rearranged because of this, am I? You start putting me between you and Matt, and he'll be after my blood."

Brooke tossed her head. "Matt James does not own me, Gary. And I'm not trying to put you between me and Matt. I just need to spend an hour or so with a friend, and you're one of the closest friends I have. If you're not interested . . ."

"Well, if you put it that way," Gary said with an au- dible smile. "Where do you want to meet?"

Brooke named one of their favorite restaurants.

"Okay. See you in a little while. I'll be the guy in the football helmet and the bulletproof vest," Gary announced cheerfully, leaving her smiling as she hung up the phone.

MATT PUSHED OPEN the door of Ribbons & Blossoms, whistling between his teeth. He'd finished a meeting at the tourist bureau earlier than he'd expected and he thought he'd surprise Brooke by taking her to lunch. He hoped she hadn't already gone, but it was only a few minutes after the time she normally left to eat.

"Hi, Rhonda," he greeted her employee cheerfully. "Brooke here?"

Rhonda frowned in mild distress. "You missed her by ten minutes. She's already gone to lunch."

"Damn. You don't know where she went, do you? Did she go home?" Maybe he could salvage something, after all. If she were at home, that meant they'd have an hour or so of total privacy. An hour or so that could be put to good use, he thought with a very masculine sense of anticipation.

"No, I don't know where she went. I only know that she was meeting Dr. Wagner someplace. She'll be sorry she missed you."

Matt swallowed the explosion that threatened to erupt from his throat. "I'm sure she will. I'll talk to her later." He would *certainly* talk to her, he thought, slamming out of the door of the florist shop he'd entered so cheerfully only a few minutes earlier.

"I'M SORRY, BROOKE. I know you don't think this is a laughing matter."

Brooke glared across the table at her grinning friend. "No, I don't."

Gary tried without much success to swallow another chuckle. "I can't help it. Wasn't it about four months ago that you tried to talk me into that very practical, carefully arranged marriage of convenience? And now here you are all in a dither because a man you happen to love has proposed to you. You have to admit it's ironic."

"*You* have to admit my plan was much less risky," Brooke said rather wistfully.

"That's because you were hiding the most vulnerable parts of yourself behind those practical, unemotional walls you tried to build. But it didn't work. Matt James came along and smashed right through those walls, and now you're just as vulnerable as the rest of us."

"I just can't get back into the same situation I had with my father, Gary. I was miserable trying to please him by repressing my own needs and desires."

"Has Matt ever asked you to be anything other than you are, Brooke? You were an independent, fully self-sufficient businesswoman when he met you. That's probably one of the things that attracted him to you. Has he ever tried to change that?"

"He's very possessive," Brooke answered cautiously. "And he wants a full accounting of everything I do."

Gary gave a twisted smile. "He's a man in love. A man in love with a woman who has made no secret of her reluctance to commit herself to him. He's probably feeling a bit insecure in your relationship. Once everything's settled, he'll probably ease off."

Brooke eyed Gary balefully. "How come you're on his side?"

"I'm not on anyone's side. But I like Matt. He's got style," Gary admitted with a grin. "And I like the look in your eyes when you talk about him. I told you you deserved to have a passionate, loving relationship. I'm glad you found it."

Brooke sighed and shook her head. "I wish I were as happy about it as everyone else seems to be. You, Rhonda, Melinda, even my father, all act as if it's so wonderful that I've fallen in love with Matt. How come I'm the only one who seems to have reservations?"

"You're the one with the most to lose," Gary replied with devastating simplicity.

Brooke moaned. "Yeah, that's what I thought."

"Cheer up, honey. It'll work out."

"I wish I had your confidence."

"I have confidence in *you*, Brooke. If you want it badly enough, you'll figure out a way to make it work."

Brooke glumly wondered if she were the only pessimist in a world full of optimists. She still had the feeling that something was about to go terribly wrong in her relationship with Matt.

BROOKE STOWED HER PURSE in her office, then turned to Rhonda. "Sorry I took so long for lunch. Gary and I talked longer than either of us realized. Any messages?"

"Matt came by just a few minutes after you left. I think he wanted to take you to lunch."

Surprised, Brooke looked up from an order sheet. "He did? I thought he was going to be busy today."

Rhonda shrugged. "He was here. And he's called twice since he left."

Brooke frowned. "Maybe something has happened that he needs to tell me about."

"If you want my opinion, I think he was just checking to see how long you were gone. I really think he didn't like it that you'd gone out with Gary for lunch."

"That's ridiculous. Matt is aware that Gary and I are just friends."

Rhonda lifted one eyebrow. "Maybe he hasn't forgotten that the first time he met you you'd just proposed marriage to this friend of yours."

Brooke flushed. "Matt knows I've put that idea behind me," she murmured gruffly.

"Does he? Or does he wonder why someone who was so all-fired eager to get married just a few months ago is so darned skittish about making that commitment to him?"

"Don't be silly." Brooke reached for the phone. "I'll call him and see what he wanted. I'm sure there was something important he wanted to tell me."

Rhonda left the room to give her employer privacy for the call.

Punching the familiar numbers, Brooke leaned back in her desk chair and waited for a response. Matt jealous of Gary? she thought with a wry smile. Rhonda's imagination was definitely getting away with her. Matt certainly had no reason to be jealous of Brooke's relationship with Gary. He knew very well that Brooke and Gary had never progressed beyond friendship. "Hi, Carol," she said gaily when Matt's secretary answered the phone. "It's Brooke. Is Matt busy?"

"Sorry, Brooke. He's out of the office, probably for several hours. There's a staff meeting this afternoon, and then Matt is speaking to a group of high-school students for a career day at their school."

Brooke had forgotten about the speech. Matt had been looking forward to that, flattered to have been asked to discuss hotel management with the young people. He'd had an extremely busy day scheduled, which was why she'd been so surprised to hear that he'd come by the shop. "Did he leave a message for me, Carol?"

"No message."

"Tell him I called, will you?"

She replaced the receiver thoughtfully, still curious about Matt's attempt to reach her while she'd been out. Then she shrugged and turned her attention to business, deciding that if it were very important Matt would find a way to contact her.

MATT WAS WAITING in her living room when she got home that evening. Since she'd given him a key, she wasn't surprised to see him, but she *was* startled by his expression. Matt James was coldly, thoroughly furious.

"Matt?" she asked cautiously. "What's wrong?"

"Have a nice lunch today?" he asked in return, leaning back against her sofa cushions in a deceptively casual pose, arms outstretched along the back of the sofa.

Oh, come on, Brooke thought in exasperation. Surely Rhonda hadn't been right about Matt being jealous of Gary. "Yes, thank you, I had a very nice lunch," she answered him, keeping her voice cool. "How was yours?"

"I didn't have lunch. I went by your shop to take you out, but it seemed that you had a previous engagement."

"Yes, well, you should have called first."

"I called twice after I got back to my office. Your lunch lasted a good two hours, didn't it, Brooke?"

"As a matter of fact, it did." She threw her purse on a chair and planted her fists on her hips, facing Matt defiantly. "All right, out with it. What's your problem this time?"

He dropped his arms and shoved himself off the sofa, stopping only a few inches away from her. "My problem," he said with icy precision, "is that I'm not crazy about finding out that the woman I love, the woman I've asked to marry me, still considers herself free to date other men."

"I do not date other men!" Brooke protested heatedly. "I had lunch with a *friend*, Matt, and I have no intention of allowing anyone—including the man I love—to choose my friends for me!"

"This *friend* is a man you were considering marrying not so very long ago," Matt almost shouted in return, unconsciously paraphrasing the words Rhonda had used earlier. "The man you'd chosen because you thought he'd make the perfect husband—remember? Compatible interests, similar goals and life-styles, an undemanding relationship. I suppose if you'd married him, you would have expected *him* to say nothing when you spent time with other men."

"I would have expected him to trust me," Brooke agreed angrily. "Which seems to be more than you do."

Matt flushed dangerously. "Still comparing us, Brooke? I don't have to be told that I come out on the short end according to your cold-blooded criteria. After all, *I'm* demanding and possessive. *I* insist that you commit yourself as fully to our relationship as I have. *I'm* not content to see you just once in a while with no questions about what you did or where you went when we were apart. *I* have no intention of waiting quietly in the wings of your life until you decide you need a convenient escort."

As furious as he was now, Brooke resisted the childish impulse to stamp her foot. "You're not being fair! I've never asked those things of you."

"Not in so many words, maybe. But don't tell me they haven't crossed your mind."

"So now you're putting words in my mind!"

He glared down at her. "Okay, tell me I'm wrong."

She tossed her head. "You're wrong."

"Then why did you run in sheer panic when I asked you to marry me? Why didn't you turn pale with terror at the thought of marrying Wagner, the way you did with me? And you claim to love me."

"I don't claim to love you!" Brooke shouted, stung by his words. "I *do* love you!"

"Why?" he demanded harshly. "Because I'm good in bed? Something about the way I look? You say you love me, but you're not sure you want to marry me. So what am I to you, Brooke? A good time between the sheets until Mr. Right comes along to fill the position of successful, undemanding, genetically suitable mate?"

Her hand shot out before she could stop it. Matt caught her wrist in an iron grip, holding her palm three inches from his face. "I've let you get away with a lot during the past few weeks," he almost snarled, "but I'll be damned if I'm going to let you hit me."

She jerked her wrist from his grasp. *"You've* let *me* get away with a lot?" she repeated incredulously, remembering all those times she'd bitten back arguments, all those incidents in which she'd allowed his high-handedness to pass without comment for the sake of peace. "Of all the arrogant, despicable, contemptible statements! It sounds exactly like something my father would have said. Dammit, I knew all along this would happen."

Matt paled, though she wasn't sure whether his reaction was deepening anger or pain at the comparison to her father. When he spoke again, his voice had lowered to deadly quiet. "You want to know what *your* problem is, Brooke?"

"Yes, Matt," she flung back at him, lifting her chin and meeting his dark glare without blinking. "I'd just love to hear what you think my problem is."

"Your problem is that you're still so hung up trying to prove something to your father that you don't even know what you want for yourself. Everything you've done for the past three years, all the accomplishments you've made—they haven't been for you. They've been for him."

"You're crazy," she said flatly.

"Am I?"

"Yes! Everything I've done for the past three years has been for *me!* And I don't see what that has to do with us, anyway."

"You're the one who said I remind you of your father. Isn't defying me just another way of proving yourself? Another way of showing that you don't need anyone in your life? That any relationship you enter into will be on your terms, with you in full control?"

"I think maybe you've spent too much time with your sister lately, Matt. Have you, perhaps, been reading her psychology textbooks? You seem to fancy yourself quite good at psychoanalysis," she jeered.

"I told you once before, I know you. I know how your mind works. And I know that you've decided it's better to break off what we have now than to take the risk that you just *might* be happy with a man you think is too much like your father!"

"I think you'd better leave now, Matt." Brooke gestured jerkily toward the door, determined that she wouldn't cry until it had closed behind him. He had started this unjustified attack; she wouldn't allow him to see that he'd hurt her terribly with his accusations.

"I think you're right. There doesn't seem to be anything left for me here." His words were low, weary, but they might as well have been barbed arrows from the impact they made on her. Flinching against the pain, she watched stiffly as he walked slowly toward the door.

Then, wanting to hurt him as much as he'd hurt her, she spoke again, just as he reached for the doorknob. "You needn't worry about the financing for your resort, Matt," she said, trying to keep her voice light, distantly mocking. "My father was quite impressed with you. I'm sure he'll be just thrilled to back you, regardless of our breakup."

"You think I give a damn about your father's money?" he asked, sounding almost stunned.

"You wouldn't be the first man who found that my most attractive feature," she threw back recklessly.

She'd wanted to hurt him; she had. The look in his eyes ripped her heart in half. Before she could blurt out the instinctive apology that formed on her lips, he was gone, leaving her haunted by the image of that look.

And she hurt. Hurt so badly that even breathing was painful. She'd thought she would cry when he left; she only wished she could. Her eyes were dry, burning with the need for tears that refused to come. Sinking onto the sofa, she stared blindly at her hands, trying to come to terms with the disaster that had just befallen her.

Matt was gone. Out of her life. She didn't try to delude herself that he'd be back this time. "There doesn't seem to be anything left for me here," he'd said, and she knew he'd meant every word.

It had come so suddenly. Funny how she'd been expecting this very explosion for so long and yet she'd been totally unprepared when it actually happened. For a moment she couldn't even remember how the fight had started.

Gary. Matt had been irate because she'd had lunch with Gary. What a trivial reason to destroy a love affair, she thought dully. Couldn't he have waited for something more important?

"He's probably feeling a bit insecure in your relationship," Gary had suggested at lunch. And Rhonda had speculated that Matt might resent Brooke seeing Gary after she'd refused to commit herself to Matt. Brooke hadn't listened to them then; it seemed she should have. She'd always thought she would be the one who'd have enough, who'd lose her temper and end the relationship. She'd always thought she'd be the one to walk out, as she had with Blake. Maybe Matt had been right about her wanting to be fully in control.

Maybe Matt was right about a lot of things. She *was* a coward; she *was* still trying to prove something to her father. And she was still afraid to take that final step and marry Matt. Even if she could mend the damage this fight had done, what if it happened again? He'd been totally unreasonable tonight, not even allowing her to defend herself. Chances were he wouldn't change. She wasn't sure she was going to survive this breakup; how much worse would it be if they'd actually been married before the end?

She thought of the practical marriage of convenience she'd conceived so long ago—back when she'd been smugly in charge of her own life, her own emotions, her heart firmly locked away. She knew now that, though it may have been a great idea, a perfect solution to her fear of getting hurt again, she'd never enter such an arrangement. The thought of being that intimate with any other man, of having children with any other man but Matt, actually turned her stomach.

He was out of her life, but he would never be out of her heart. And she didn't for the life of her know what she was going to do about it.

She was actually relieved when the tears finally burst sometime during the endless, sleepless night. At least they gave her something to do besides lie awake and desperately miss Matt.

"KIND OF LATE getting home, aren't you?" Melinda asked Matt, barely looking up as he entered the living room of his suite.

"What are you doing still up?" he asked, his voice sounding raw and rusty even to him.

"I got involved in a late movie. It's just finished. I take it you've been with Brooke?" Melinda did look at her brother then; she gasped at what she saw. "My God, Matt, what happened? What's wrong?"

He lifted his hands in an expressive gesture of hopelessness. "Brooke and I split up. It's over."

Her green eyes widening in shock, Melinda caught her brother's hands in hers. "Surely not. You've had a quarrel, but you'll make up. I know you will. You love each other."

"I love her, but we won't make up this time. It's really over."

Melinda blinked back sympathetic tears. "Oh, Matt. Surely you don't believe she doesn't love you? I just know she does."

"Maybe," he answered tonelessly. "But it wasn't enough. She's been looking for a reason to end it since our first date. Tonight I gave her a reason."

"What did you do?"

"I yelled at her for having lunch with her friend Gary. I don't really know why I went so berserk. Maybe I was just tired of waiting for the ax to fall. Maybe I just wanted to force the issue, to get it over with. Maybe I was hoping I was wrong, hoping she'd tell me that I had nothing to worry about with her and Gary because she loved only me. That she wanted to accept my proposal, to be a real, permanent part of my life, just as I wanted to be in hers. But she didn't say any of that. She told me that I had no right to choose her friends, told me that she knew all along we weren't going to make it and finally accused me of caring more about her father's money than I did about her."

Appalled, Melinda raised her hands to her cheeks. "Oh, Matt, she didn't! Lord, I didn't even know her father *had* money."

He shrugged. "She told me a long time ago that she was from a wealthy family, but I never thought much about it. Actually I think I was taking the blame for some other guy on that one. Someone who'd hurt her in the past. If I thought she really believed that I'd care more about money than her—" He stopped, his jaw clenching in a wave of pain.

Why? he asked himself with the dull ache of weary depression. Why hadn't she given them a chance? Why had she been so very eager to seize the first chance to end it? And why had he been so hell-bent to offer that chance?

Maybe it was best, he told himself, turning away from the unhappiness in Melinda's eyes. Maybe it was just as well that it had ended now. He'd known from the moment he'd proposed that Brooke didn't intend to marry him. Just as he'd known that he wouldn't be able to go on indefinitely seeing her only when she had time for him. He wanted a wife, not an occasional lover. He wanted Brooke. But he hadn't been able to offer her ideal of a workable marriage. He wanted a real marriage, based on passion and emotion and deep, lasting love, not a cold, modern business arrangement complete with prenuptial agreements and formal conditions.

He had to accept that it was over. Had to learn to go on, somehow, without her. But he wasn't sure he'd survive intact. Something deep inside him had already died.

Choking down a cry of rage and pain, he turned abruptly and headed for the dark privacy of his own room. He didn't see the look of speculative determination that crossed Melinda's face as she watched him walk away.

12

BROOKE SCRAPED a full plate of food into the garbage disposal and rinsed the dish, listlessly placing it in the dishwasher. She'd thought she was hungry when she'd prepared the light luncheon; she'd realized when she'd sat down to eat that she wasn't. Not that she was surprised. She hadn't been hungry since she and Matt had broken up, nine days earlier.

Wandering into her living room, she trailed her fingertips along the furniture she passed and wondered what she'd do with herself for the rest of the day. It was Sunday, so the shop was closed. Her paperwork was caught up, the apartment had been scrubbed until it practically glittered and books and television didn't particularly interest her just then. She'd stayed as busy as possible during the past nine days, trying to avoid a time like this when she had nothing to do but miss Matt.

Swallowing a moan at the thought of him, she wondered despairingly how long she could go on like this, missing him, aching for him, asking herself if she'd been wrong to let him leave. Surely she could have done something to make him stay, said something that would have solved all their problems. Couldn't she have, if she'd really tried?

She was so tired of the what-ifs. So tired of asking herself whose fault the breakup had been, wondering if she'd been wrong to resist falling in love with him or if she'd been right all along in insisting that she and Matt had no future together.

She hadn't seen him since he'd walked out of her apartment, though she'd talked to Melinda a couple of times on the telephone. Melinda had said little about the breakup, though she'd complained that Matt was harder to live with than ever, his temper dangerously short fused. Brooke wondered if he could possibly be hurting as badly as she was. Could he love her so much that each hour without her was another hour of torment? she wondered with tears brimming in her eyes. What had they done to each other?

She jumped when her doorbell rang. Her heart pounded in her throat. Was it Matt? And if so, should she coolly send him away, knowing she was doing the right thing in the long run, or should she follow her instincts and throw herself in his arms, begging him never to leave her again?

It wasn't Matt. Melinda stood outside Brooke's door, her young face a portrait of tragedy, her eyes redrimmed from crying. "Melinda!" Brooke gasped, drawing the teenager inside the apartment. "What's wrong?"

"Matt . . . Matt and I had a terrible fight," Melinda confessed, her voice breaking pitifully. "He . . . he fired me from my job."

"He did *what*?" Brooke asked in a near squeak, staring at the visibly devastated young woman in front of her. "Why would he do that?"

"All I did was express my honest opinion about a particular situation at the hotel and he lost his temper completely," Melinda answered in a broken whisper. "He yelled at me and told me he was sick of dealing with me. And then he told me that he wanted me on a plane to Springfield tonight."

Brooke could hardly believe her ears. She'd known Matt had a temper, of course, and she'd known that he and Melinda didn't always get along. But she would never have guessed that he'd be cruel enough to put his younger sister in such a state. What could he have said that was so horrible that even Melinda's brash spirit was broken?

"You poor kid," Brooke crooned, taking Melinda in her arms.

Melinda sobbed quietly into Brooke's sympathetic shoulder. "I don't know what I'm going to do, Brooke. I only have three weeks left to work, and I needed the money I would have made. There's not time now to find another job in Springfield before school starts. No one would hire me for only three weeks. And I can't bear the thought of going home in disgrace, earlier than I'd planned to return."

Brooke wondered why Melinda needed three more weeks' salary so badly; she'd understood that money was not a problem in Melinda's family. And she thought going home in disgrace was rather a dramatic way of referring to the situation. But then Melinda gave another wrenching sob, and Brooke's tender heart twisted. "Don't cry, Melinda. If you really want to work for the next three weeks, you can work for me. I can always use extra help around the shop. It won't be as glamorous as working at the Amber Rose, of course. You'll be working in jeans and T-shirts, your hands in potting soil as often as not."

"I wouldn't mind that. Would you let me stay here with you? I don't have anyplace to stay now that Matt's thrown me out."

"Of course you can stay with me," Brooke assured her, her anger with Matt flaring again at Melinda's description of his treatment of her. "We'll have to get your things, of course, but then—"

"Oh, that's okay. I've already got my things," Melinda replied, her tears miraculously dried. Smiling brightly, she hugged Brooke hard. "Glenn's downstairs, waiting in his car. He brought me over. My bags are in his trunk."

Blinking, Brooke followed Melinda toward the door. "Uh, Melinda?" she began hesitantly, but she was talking to an empty doorway.

Half an hour later Melinda was happily settled in Brooke's spare bedroom. Visibly infatuated with the young woman, Glenn had carried in her bags, then left after making her promise to call him if she needed him. "This is going to be fun," Melinda told Brooke cheerfully, her hands clasped in front of her. "We can be like roommates!"

"Yes, it'll be fun," Brooke echoed, trying to keep the doubt out of her voice as she wondered at the wisdom of agreeing to allow Melinda to live and work with her for the next three weeks. "Melinda, did you tell Matt you were coming here?"

Melinda tossed her thick strawberry-blond hair over the shoulder of her electric-blue T-shirt, her nose tilted upward. "No. He stormed out and I packed and left while he was gone. He won't know where I am."

"You'd better call him. He'll be worried."

"He won't care where I am," Melinda argued dramatically. "He doesn't care what happens to me as long as I'm out of his way now."

"Now, Melinda, that isn't true. I know Matt's angry with you now, but he loves you. You know that."

Melinda scowled. "Matt doesn't love *anyone*. Just that all-powerful job of his. All he wants to do is boss people around and have them bow down to him. Isn't that why *you* broke up with him? That was a smart thing to do, Brooke. I never did understand what you saw in him."

"Melinda, you're not being fair," Brooke protested. "Of course Matt loves you. He loves you very much."

Melinda's chin set stubbornly. "I won't call him. If he's really worried about me, then it serves him right."

"I'll have to call him, then. I'm sorry, Melinda, but I can't let him worry needlessly."

"What do you care about whether he's worried or not?" Melinda asked, sounding genuinely confused. "Brooke, he treated you like dirt. You should be glad that everything's not going his way for a change."

Exasperated with the convoluted workings of the teenage mind, Brooke pushed back her hair and tried to speak calmly. "Melinda, Matt did *not* treat me like dirt. There were many reasons our relationship didn't work out, but none of them is important right now. I'm going to call him and tell him where you are."

"Suit yourself," Melinda said with a shrug. "I'm going to unpack."

How do I get myself into these messes? Brooke wondered even as she picked up the telephone with a hand that was not quite steady. Her chest felt tight as she dialed Matt's number, a number she hadn't planned to dial again, though many times during the past nine days she'd caught herself staring longingly at the telephone, her fingers itching to push these same buttons. Matt picked up on the first ring. "Melinda?" he demanded without preamble. "Where the hell—"

"Matt, it's Brooke," Brooke interrupted hastily.

There was a stunned pause, and then he spoke again, his voice quite different this time. "Brooke?"

"Yes, I . . . I just called to tell you that Melinda is with me. I didn't want you to worry about her."

Matt sighed gustily. "I should have known she'd go to you. Listen, you don't have to bother with her. I'll come get her."

"No, you won't," Brooke answered firmly. "She's asked to stay with me for the next three weeks, and I've agreed."

"You did *what*?"

"She doesn't want to be sent home like a child in trouble. She says she would be humiliated, and I can't really blame her. I told her she could stay here until she had planned to return to Springfield. She's going to help me out around the shop, as well."

"Brooke, I know you're trying to help, but you don't understand what's going on. She's using you to get back at me, that's all. Don't let her put you in the middle."

Brooke stiffened, her chin squaring. "And what was I supposed to do when she showed up crying on my doorstep, Matt? Throw her out on the street? She was devastated by the way you treated her!"

"The way *I* treated *her*?" Matt repeated with apparent disbelief. "Just what the hell did she tell you?"

"That you'd fired her from her job at the Amber Rose and that you intended to put her on a plane to Springfield tonight. She was heartbroken. You had no right to take your anger with me out on your innocent little sister, Matt. It wasn't fair."

Matt was silent for a long time, but Brooke could almost hear the waves of temper pounding through the telephone line. "All right, fine," he said at last, the words grated out between clenched teeth. "If you want to try to handle my innocent younger sister for the next three weeks, then be my guest. Just let her loose on *your* place of business and watch the results. It will give me great pleasure to say I told you so when you come running to me to get her out of your hair!"

"When I—" Brooke choked on her rage. "Why, you . . . you arrogant worm! I wouldn't come running to you if— Well, I just won't!" she finished almost incoherently. "This is the gratitude I get for trying to keep you from worrying about Melinda! I'm beginning to believe she's right. You *don't* care about anyone!"

"Always ready to believe the worst of me, aren't you, Brooke? To condemn without even hearing my side. Since you're already so convinced I'm a heartless, pompous bastard, I don't suppose it will make any difference if I do *this*." And with that, he slammed the phone down in her ear, so hard she winced at the crash.

She pulled her own receiver away to stare at it, her mouth half open.

"I told you not to call him," Melinda observed placidly from the doorway to the guest room.

"He hung up on me!" Brooke said in incredulous fury. "He actually hung up on me."

Melinda shrugged. "That's Matt. So what do you want to do for the rest of the afternoon? How about a trip to the mall?"

BY THE END of the first week with Melinda, Brooke was beginning to feel a bit . . . frazzled. Melinda seemed to have very definite ideas on just about every subject—running a business among them. More than once Brooke had to step in to stop an all-out revolt among her employees when Melinda blithely gave "advice" to various people about improving their job performance. It also took a great deal of patience to endure Melinda's tendency to say whatever happened to cross her rather eccentric mind. Brooke found it very hard to understand why she especially resented Melinda's frequent, vitriolic attacks on Matt. More and more, Brooke found herself defending him, making Melinda wonder aloud why Brooke felt it necessary to take Matt's side when they were no longer even seeing each other. Dealing with Melinda, in addition to dealing with her own stubborn longing for Matt, had Brooke a weary bundle of nerves by the Saturday after Melinda moved in.

Melinda had asked permission for Lynette and Sherry to visit that evening, and Brooke had agreed, thinking it might be fun to spend a few hours with the lively teenagers. Somewhat nostalgically, she thought of similar evenings in her own home in Denver. Her mother had always provided delicious snacks for Brooke and her friends, never seeming to mind the loud giggles and frequent squeals from the boisterous young people, nor the occasional "raids" of teenage boys.

Since she'd worked most of the day, Brooke didn't have time to prepare anything special for her guests, but she did encourage them to order an enormous pizza with everything as her treat. The three younger women begged Brooke to join them for dinner, which she did gratefully, relieved to have an excuse not to mope over Matt. It turned out to be quite impossible, however, to totally forget about Matt during the next few hours. At Melinda's instigation, the topic turned frequently to Matt as all three of the teenagers seemed to find great pleasure in slicing Matt's character to shreds.

"Lynette!" Brooke protested after one such poisonous barb. "I thought you liked Matt!"

"Oh, I did," the blue-eyed brunette assured her, "until I found out what a hateful bully he is. It was just criminal the way he treated Melinda."

"Lynette, a bully is someone who habitually abuses those who are smaller or weaker than himself," Brooke pointed out. "Matt isn't really a bully."

"He's a jerk," Sherry announced with relish. "Boy, I'm glad *I* don't have a brother like that. Poor Melinda, I don't know how you've stood it all these years."

"And to think you almost married him," Melinda added to Brooke. "I guess you really feel lucky to be out of that relationship, don't you?"

"Well, I—"

"Ooh, can you imagine being *married* to him?" Lynette asked with an exaggerated shudder. "It would be awful! He'd probably be a wife beater or something."

"Lynette!"

Ignoring Brooke's reprimand, Melinda laughed and agreed with her friend. "Can't you hear him now? 'I'm home, woman! Where's my dinner? And don't give me any backtalk! Nobody asked for your opinion!'"

Lynette and Sherry dissolved into helpless giggles at Melinda's wicked imitation. Brooke pushed her plate aside and stood, flushed with irritation at the three of them. "If you'll excuse me, I'm going to my room to read for a while. And I think you should all be ashamed of yourselves for being so cruel to someone who has been very good to all of you!"

Not even bothering to ask herself why she was so angry with the girls for their juvenile attacks on Matt, Brooke stormed out of the kitchen. A moment of silence followed her and then another outburst of giggling.

Teenagers! she thought with displeasure, wondering how her mother had ever managed to be so gracious to Brooke's friends.

BLESSEDLY ALONE for a few hours on Sunday afternoon while Melinda went swimming with her friends, Brooke decided to call her mother. She tried to call every so often, anyway, and she'd had the urge to talk to her mother ever since Lynette and Sherry's visit had reminded her of her own girlhood. "Mom? Hi, it's Brooke."

"Brooke! How nice to hear from you. How are you, dear?"

"I'm fine, Mother. How about you?"

"Oh, I'm fine, too. Your father enjoyed seeing you earlier this month. I'm glad the two of you got along so well. He's hoping that you'll come home for a visit soon."

Brooke blinked in surprise. Her father had thought they'd gotten along well? Perhaps, compared to their stormy past, they'd managed well enough, but she'd have hardly called the visit a blazing success.

"He was very impressed with your new boyfriend, Matt. He told me all about him," Olivia continued blandly. "He was a bit miffed that Matt turned down his offer to invest in Matt's new resort, but I think Nathan rather admired your young man's independent streak."

Brooke's fingers tightened on the receiver. "Matt turned down Dad's offer?" she repeated weakly.

"You didn't know?" Olivia asked in surprise. "Nathan offered to set Matt up in his new business, but Matt told him that he had already arranged other financing. I believe he also said that he thought it was best for family not to get mixed up in business together. In other words, he didn't want to be indebted to his future father-in-law. Nathan was rather amused by that."

"Mother, Matt and I—" Brooke hesitated, wondering how to explain that Matt had been overly optimistic in hinting that he and Brooke were to be married.

"Oh, I know. Nathan said it was obvious you were very much in love. I know your father doesn't express his feelings easily, Brooke, but he's pleased that you're happy. And he's quite proud of the success you've made of your flower shop. You should hear him bragging about you to our friends."

"Bragging about me?" Brooke echoed, her voice choked in disbelief.

"Oh, my, yes. You'd think you were the president of General Motors or something. He's told everyone how you started your business on a shoestring and turned it into a paying venture. He's even told them that you'll own a whole chain of florists soon. Claims he taught you everything you know and called you a chip off the old block. It's very sweet, really," Olivia added, her voice thickening with emotion.

"I, uh, I'm surprised," Brooke admitted, and knew she was drastically understating.

"Oh, Brooke, we miss you very much. Please try to visit us soon. And bring that young man of yours. I do so want to meet him."

"We'll talk about it later, Mother," Brooke promised, unable to go into long explanations just then, with so much else to think about. Her father was *proud* of her?

Matt had turned down her father's offer of financial backing. Brooke winced as she paced restlessly around her apartment, remembering her accusation that he'd been as interested in her father's money as he had been in her. That had been unfair of her. She'd been hurt and angry at Matt—and she still believed herself justified, particularly now after his fight with Melinda—but she shouldn't have lashed out at him for something another man had done to her.

"What am I going to do?" she asked aloud, hearing the dejection in her voice. She'd been so afraid of being unhappy with Matt; she was utterly miserable without him. She wanted so desperately to go to him, to rashly agree to anything to keep him in her life, but . . . what if he no longer wanted her? He hadn't been exactly encouraging the last time she'd talked to him. And had anything really changed? Look at the way he'd treated his own sister. What was to stop him from making Brooke just as unhappy as he'd made Melinda?

"Oh, Matt," she moaned, hiding her face in her hands, "why do I love you this much? What is it about you that won't let me get over you?"

SWEAT POURING OFF his barely clad body, Matt draped a white towel around his neck and reached for a cool glass of orange juice. Throwing back his head, he greedily guzzled the refreshing beverage, draining the glass before setting it down. Absently swiping at the drops of perspiration dampening his bare chest, he stared morosely at the physical training equipment he'd just attacked with what was becoming habitual determination. He'd spent a lot of time in the workout room during the past two weeks, trying to exhaust his body, which still ached for Brooke. No other woman could have eased the pain of wanting her; the hours of working himself to quivery jelly were having no noticeable effect, either.

He wanted her. He needed her. He missed her so much he was going insane. But he wouldn't go to her, begging her to take him back. She'd been so ready to end it, so eager to believe the worst of him in every situation. He couldn't live with that, couldn't take the constant insecurity of wondering when she would decide to call it quits again. If ever they were to be together, he had to know that she was as fully committed to making it work as he was.

Hitching up the brief blue shorts that were his only garment other than a pair of white sneakers, he ran his other hand through his damp hair and wondered how Brooke was getting along full-time with Melinda. If only she'd asked for Matt's side of the story... But again, she'd been too ready to accept the worst. He only hoped Melinda would pull some of the same stunts with Brooke that she'd tried on Matt during the week after Matt and Brooke had broken up. It was almost as if she'd dared him to do anything about it. She'd finally pushed him to the point that he had lost his temper. Hell, a saint would have lost his temper at that point! Matt thought with self-righteous indignation.

Maybe Brooke would find out for herself that living with Melinda was hardly the easiest task in the world.

Brooke. He almost moaned as his body reacted immediately to the thought of her name. Sighing deeply, he tugged the towel off his neck and headed grimly toward the slant board. Maybe a few more sit-ups . . .

"A DOZEN RED ROSES?" Melinda asked the stern-faced gentleman with audible scorn. "That's so unoriginal. Can't you think of anything more interesting to send your wife for your anniversary?"

"Melinda!" Brooke said in a gasp, having been close enough to overhear. "Excuse me, sir," she told the scowling customer. "Melinda, wait for me in the back, please." Backing up the order with a glare, Brooke turned apologetically to the displeased man. "A dozen red roses is a lovely gift for an anniversary," she assured him. "Most women adore them. Please forgive my young employee. She's . . . well, she's a little unconventional, I'm afraid."

Having soothed the gentleman's offended sensibilities, Brooke stepped determinedly into the back room. It was time to stop avoiding the issue with Melinda, she decided. The young woman's behavior had been progressively more outrageous, but insulting the customers was going too far. "Melinda, we have to talk," she began the moment she joined the sullen young woman.

"You're mad at me, aren't you?" Melinda demanded, chin lifted in defiance.

"As a matter of fact, I am. Surely you know better than to speak to a customer in that manner. I can't afford to offend my customers, Melinda, regardless of your opinion of their taste in flowers."

"Are you firing me?"

Startled at the belligerent question, Brooke blinked. "Melinda, I—"

"Okay, fine!" Melinda almost shouted. "Fire me! No one cares about me, anyway. You and Matt deserve each other. You're just alike!" And with that, she stormed out of the shop.

Brooke started to follow but was delayed by a telephone call that required her attention. By the time she'd completed the call, Melinda had gone. Assuming she'd go to Brooke's place to cool off, Brooke decided to wait until they'd both calmed down before trying to reason with Melinda. She had already decided that she may have been too hard on Matt concerning his relationship with his thoroughly exasperating sister.

MELINDA WASN'T at Brooke's apartment, nor was there any evidence that she'd been there since they'd left for work that morning. Sighing, Brooke called her friends. "Lynette, I'm looking for Melinda. Is she there?"

"Why, no," Lynette replied. "You mean you don't know where she is?"

"No. Call me if you hear from her, will you, Lynette?"

"Of course."

Chewing her lip, Brooke hung up the phone. Where else could Melinda have gone? she wondered. She hadn't made that many friends in Nashville, or at least not that Brooke knew of. She'd give her a little while longer, then try again to find her.

By eight o'clock Brooke was worried. She'd called Lynette again, only to be told that the girls still hadn't heard from Melinda. Nor had Glenn, who'd dated her a few times. "I'm worried about her," Lynette told Brooke. "Maybe you'd better go tell Matt that she's missing."

"Yes, I suppose I'd better," Brooke conceded. "Call over there if you hear anything, okay?"

Twenty minutes later Brooke stood outside Matt's door. It had been seventeen days—she'd counted— since she'd seen Matt, and though her reason for being here had nothing to do with their own troubled relationship, she still trembled at the thought of knocking on his door. She'd almost called him, but decided that approach was too cowardly. After all, she had lost his little sister. She owed him a personal explanation. Drawing a deep breath for courage, she lifted a hand and tapped briskly on the door.

13

MATT LOOKED STUNNED to see her. "Brooke?"

For an unguarded moment she thought she saw pure joy in his eyes, but then he shuttered the expression and stepped aside to invite her in. Her heart pounding at what she'd seen in his eyes—at what she felt in her own heart at seeing him again—she entered his suite, her hands clenched into damp fists. Lord, he looked wonderful, she thought wistfully. Had she really forgotten how truly handsome he was, or had she simply refused to allow herself to remember? "Matt, I . . . I have to tell you something."

He seemed to steel himself for her words. "What is it?" he asked, his voice carefully impassive.

"I've . . . I've lost Melinda," she admitted in a rush, eyeing him warily for his reaction.

Whatever he'd expected, it obviously hadn't been that. "You've what?"

"She got very angry with me and stormed out of the shop. That was at three o'clock this afternoon, and I haven't seen her since. I've called Lynette and Sherry, and they don't know where she is, nor does Glenn. I don't know what to do, Matt. I don't know where she could have gone."

Matt stared at her for a long, frozen moment, then grinned. And then he was laughing. "I knew it," he said, managing to bring his voice under control. "I knew it wouldn't last."

Glaring indignantly at him, she planted her fists on her hips. "Matt, didn't you hear me? She's missing! I don't know where she is. I'm worried about her."

"Melinda is nineteen, Brooke. She's perfectly capable of taking care of herself. In fact, she's probably with Lynette and Sherry."

"But they—"

"Do you really think they'd tell you she was there if she'd asked them not to?"

She bit her lip and shook her head. "No. They'd probably consider it their duty to be loyal to their friend, especially if she'd told them that I—"

"That you what?" Matt prodded, crossing his arms in front of him.

"That I'd lost my temper and fired her," Brooke finished reluctantly. "She probably exaggerated . . ."

Her voice trailed off as she realized what she'd said. "Oh, Matt."

He only looked at her, his expression unreadable.

"Matt, please tell me what happened between you and Melinda."

He lifted one brow. "You mean you want to hear *my* side?"

"Yes. Please."

He tilted his head, seeming to consider her request, then shrugged. "She pushed me over the edge—deliberately, I think. The final straw came when I caught her trying to organize a strike among the housekeeping staff. She told them they should demand more money and better working conditions, even though they already have excellent benefits and wages comparable to the same position with any other hotel in the state."

Brooke groaned. "A strike?"

"Yes. She even made signs accusing me of practicing slave labor. She was lucky I fired her instead of turning her over my knee in front of the entire staff. Maybe I should have."

"She didn't tell me any of that," Brooke admitted.

He made no effort to hide the hurt in his eyes then. "Would you have believed her if she had? You may have actually had to admit that I was justified in my actions."

"Matt, I'm sorry," Brooke whispered, blinking back tears. "I should have asked for your side of the story. I had already decided before I came here tonight that I was wrong to jump to conclusions. Now that I've had to live with Melinda myself for over a week, I know you haven't had an easy time with her this summer."

Matt inhaled sharply at the sight of her tears, then let the breath out in a hard gust and caught her into his arms. Burying his face in her hair, he ground out, "Dammit, Brooke, why did you have to come here tonight? God, don't you know how much I've missed you, how much I've wanted to hold you? I've been going crazy without you. I don't know if I can let you go again."

Brooke clung to Matt's shirt, burrowing into the solid warmth of his shoulder. "Oh, Matt, I've missed you, too. I've been so miserable during the past weeks. Please don't let me go."

He tugged insistently at a fistful of curls, pulling her face up to his. "I love you," he muttered, covering her mouth with his before she could answer in kind.

The kiss was deep, measureless, desperate. All the pain, all the need, all the overpowering love inside them came out in that embrace, leaving them both bruised and panting when it finally ended.

Matt dropped his hands on Brooke's shoulders and held her firmly only a few inches away from him, his jaw set with determination, leaf-green eyes sparkling dangerously. "I've had it with your cowardice, Brooke Matheny. It's time we got this settled, once and for all. Don't you see how ridiculous it is for us to be miserable apart simply because you're afraid we might not always be happy together? What does it take to get it through your head that we belong together? We're getting married, Brooke, and dammit, we're going to make it work! And I don't want to hear any of your petty arguments, do you understand?"

Fighting back a smile, Brooke nodded. "Yes, Matt."

He eyed her suspiciously. "Yes, what?"

"Yes, I'll marry you. But not because you're ordering me to do so," she added with a stern look at him. "You're a bossy, possessive, thick-skulled man, Matthew James, and I refuse to put up with your petty tantrums, do you understand? You may be supreme ruler of the Amber Rose, but I've seen you in your underwear."

Matt lifted an eyebrow, looking puzzled by her words. "You've what?"

"It doesn't matter now," she told him airily, deciding to talk to him later about the chat she'd had with Melinda. "I'm marrying you, Matt, knowing it won't always be easy, because nothing could be worse than trying to live without you. I never want to be that unhappy again."

His eyes lightened, but he hesitated when he would have pulled her into his arms. "You're sure?" he prodded. "I'll admit I can be overbearing and possessive. At times," he qualified. "But I'm not," he added sternly, "as bad as your father. Surely you have to admit that."

"No," she agreed, "you're not my father. And besides, unlike my mother, I'm rather stubborn and strong-willed myself. I can hold my own with you."

"I won't settle for an impersonal, businesslike marriage with you," he warned. "I want a real marriage—for better, for worse, in sickness and health, et cetera, et cetera."

"That's what I want, too," she assured him. "A real marriage with you. With love and passion and children."

"We'll quarrel sometimes."

"And we'll make up. Every time. I love you, Matt."

She seemed to have found the words he needed to reassure him that she knew what she was doing. Groaning deep in his chest, he hauled her back against him, ravaging her mouth with victorious satisfaction. She answered kiss for kiss, her arms locked around his neck, her body pressed to his rapidly hardening one. Desire flamed through her, making itself felt in her swelling breasts and that deep, hidden part of her that dampened and burned with need for him.

His hand moved to the back zipper of her dress. A sudden rush of cool air against her back cleared her thoughts. She gasped and stiffened in his arms. "Matt, we can't! Not until we find Melinda."

He groaned in protest. "I need you, Brooke. It's been so long."

She looked up at him beseechingly. "Oh, Matt, I want you, too, but we have to know for certain that she's all right."

He sighed. "I'll call Smitty's. Lynette won't lie to *me*."

The telephone rang before he reached it. "What do you want to bet that's Melinda?" he asked Brooke with a rueful grimace. He lifted the receiver to his ear. "Matt James."

Brooke knew it was Melinda when Matt scowled. "Where have you been?" he demanded. "Don't you know how worried Brooke has been about you? Yes, she's here."

He listened for a moment, then said flatly, "You *should* be sorry. I'm used to your shenanigans, but Brooke didn't deserve it. All right, you can stay there tonight, but I'd better see you here by noon tomorrow, you got that?

"She's with Lynette and Sherry," he told Brooke when he'd replaced the receiver. "She's spending the night with them. She told me to tell you that she's sorry she behaved so badly this afternoon and she hopes you'll forgive her."

"I'm just glad she's all right," Brooke answered fervently.

He frowned thoughtfully. "Something isn't right. Melinda's been acting weird, even for her."

Brooke smiled and stepped closer to him, her hands sliding up his chest. "Now that we know she's okay, perhaps we could get back to where we were earlier. You do remember where we left off, don't you?"

Willingly distracted, he smiled down at her. "Oh, I remember. I'd be happy to demonstrate."

"Please do," she encouraged him, going up on her tiptoes to press her mouth to his.

She laughed as he immediately swept her off her feet and into his arms. His grin was piratical when he looked down at her. "Too late to change your mind now, lady. I'm going to make you so thoroughly mine tonight that you'll never try to get away from me again."

"That works both ways, you know," she murmured in response, her arms locking around his neck.

"Sweetheart, I've been yours since that first day I saw you in that restaurant." He groaned, holding her closer. Turning on one heel, he moved toward his bedroom.

She didn't quite know how he managed it, but he had her clothes off almost before he placed her on the bed. She only hoped the garments would be in one piece when she put them back on later, but at the moment that was a very small concern, indeed. She promptly forgot it.

Stripping out of his own clothes, Matt came to her in a rush of need, his hands and mouth racing over her body as if to reacquaint him with the beloved territory. And then he slowed, wanting to take his time, lying half over her as he kissed her. He made love to her mouth with his, his tongue thrusting slowly, deeply inside in a pale imitation of the possession to follow. Her fingers stabbing into his rich brown hair, Brooke opened to him, her tongue joining his in a leisurely dance of love. Their bodies pressed tightly together but not moving, they kissed again and again, stopping only to draw ragged, simultaneous breaths or to move their heads to explore a new angle.

At long last, kissing wasn't enough for either of them. Matt dragged his mouth down her cheek to her throat where he nipped and licked at the glistening hollow there before moving downward toward her invitingly upthrust breasts. He pressed his lips to the upward swell of one swollen mound, then nibbled a tantalizing path across her chest, coming close to but never touching her hardened nipples. Brooke growled her frustration with his taunting and tightened her fingers in his hair, holding his head as she pushed herself upward.

Matt stroked the tip of his tongue over one pointed tip, making her shiver helplessly at the warm, wet feel of him. "Is this what you want, sweetheart?" he murmured huskily, smiling against her skin.

"Yes! Oh, Matt," she whispered as he finally relented and took her into his mouth. He loved her with his hands and teeth and tongue, first one breast and then the other, until she was arching rhythmically beneath him, burning to complete the embrace. Her hands slid down his back to his thighs, then moved inward, seeking him. Matt groaned when she found him, lifting himself to better accommodate her touch. Moments later he, too, was shuddering with the need for release.

Murmuring almost incoherent love words, he lifted himself over her and thrust forward, burying himself deeply within her. Brooke cried out with pleasure at the union, arching to take him deeper. His hands locked in her tumbled curls, Matt stilled and looked down at her, and his smile was so warm, so tender that her eyes flooded with tears. "I love you," he said, his own eyes suspiciously bright.

"Oh, Matt, I love you. I love you so much." She pulled his head down to hers.

The kiss was a slow, sweet sealing of vows, an emotional joining as real, as thorough as their physical union. And then Matt moved, rocking against her, rebuilding their passion to a frenzied peak. Release came in a burst of ecstasy, signaled by delirious, simultaneous cries of pleasure.

"You'll marry me?" Matt asked again, when he could speak coherently.

"Yes." She nestled deeper into his shoulder. "I'll marry you."

"Can you take some time off next week?"

She lifted her head, eyes wide. "You want to get married next *week*?"

He grinned. "I'd marry you tonight if I could. I want you so tied to me that it'll take an act of God for you to get out of it."

"I'm not going to try to get out of it, Matt."

"Damned right, you're not. Anyway, I thought we could take Melinda back to Springfield at the end of next week and be married there. I'd like to have my family at the wedding."

Her head spinning a bit, Brooke swallowed and nodded. "Okay. Next week."

"You're sure?" Again that trace of vulnerability, always so startling in Matt, showed in his eyes as he asked the question.

Brooke lifted a hand to his cheek. "I'm sure. And would you mind if I called my parents and asked them to join us? I'd like them to be there, too."

"I'm glad," Matt said simply. "We'll call Merry tomorrow and have her make all the arrangements. She's good at that sort of thing."

Pulling her lower lip between her teeth, Brooke hung her head guiltily. "Matt, what I said about my father's money. . . I'm sorry. I know that never meant anything to you."

"It meant something to that other guy—the one you were involved with before?"

"It meant everything to him."

Matt rolled to loom over her, pushing her onto her back beneath him. "I don't give a damn about your father's money, Brooke. I turned down his offer of financing. I decided there would probably be too many strings attached."

"I know you did. My mother told me," she admitted. "And you're probably right. Dad would want to be involved in your business. But, Matt—"

"I don't need his financing, sweetheart," he told her gently. "Ken and I have already found a backer. We start the resort next spring."

"Oh, Matt, that's wonderful! I'm so proud of you." She reached up to hug him warmly.

"Thanks. It may not be easy at first, just getting started and all. But I think we can make a success of it."

"I know you can. And I'm not bad at business myself, if you ever need any advice," she said with a cocky grin.

"That's why I'm marrying you, of course," he returned without a pause, "for your business experience."

"And I thought it was because of my fresh carrot cake."

"That, too." He slid his hand slowly down her bare side. "Among other things."

"Mm." She squirmed happily under his touch.

His eyes darkened. "I want you again, Brooke. It seemed that we were apart for months."

"I know. I missed you so much, Matt. Sometimes I thought I'd just curl up and die."

"Sometimes I wanted to." He lowered his mouth to kiss her lingeringly, his hand easing around to cup one breast.

Brooke inhaled sharply, amazed that her desire had returned full force, and so quickly. "Oh, Matt."

Just as she'd begun to lose herself in his lovemaking, Matt groaned and fell back on the bed. Gasping a protest, Brooke lifted her head and stared at him. "Matt? What's wrong?"

Grimacing ruefully, he looked at her. "I have to make an apology."

"Darling, can't it wait?"

One side of his mouth quirked upward at the plaintive wail, but he shook his head resolutely. "No. You made your apology. Now I have to make mine. I'm sorry I yelled at you for having lunch with your friend. And, even though I'm a rather possessive type overall, I won't stop you from having male friends. As long," he qualified sternly, "as you're not planning on marrying any of them."

She smiled and leaned over him. "Now how could I do that if I'm already married to you?"

"And no kissing them," he added.

She touched her lips to his and spoke against them. "Now why would I do that when you're the only man I want to kiss?"

"And definitely," he murmured, his voice growing husky, "no making love with anyone but me. Ever."

"Now why should I do that when there's no one else in the world I'd rather make love with?" She eased herself down to lie fully on top of him, her mouth coming down firmly on his.

When the kiss finally ended, Matt drew back only to mutter, "Just so you know the rules," then pulled her back down to him.

BROOKE WOKE ABRUPTLY the next morning to the sound of a delighted squeal. "You're back together! I *knew* it!"

"For God's sake, Melinda!" Matt shoved himself upright, making sure Brooke was discreetly covered. Shoving his hand through his rumpled hair, he glared at his beaming sister. "What are you doing in here?"

Melinda tossed her head and leaned against the doorway, grinning broadly. "I just wanted to tell you I'm home. Good morning, Brooke."

Fighting down a blush, Brooke cleared her throat. "Good morning, Melinda." She was a bit startled to see that none of Melinda's anger seemed to linger from the day before; the young woman looked outright smug. "You're, uh, you're not mad at me now?"

Melinda giggled. "I was never mad at you, Brooke. But I thought I was *never* going to get you to lose your temper with me! You're a lot slower to lose your temper than Matt is, you know."

Frowning in confusion, Brooke struggled to sit up, making sure the bedclothes covered her to her throat. "You *wanted* to make me lose my temper with you?"

"I knew it. Dammit, Brooke, we've been manipulated!" Matt muttered in disgust.

"By an expert," Melinda agreed cockily. "It was something my first boyfriend, Savage, taught me—give two opponents a common enemy and they'll band together. Looks to me like you two are together."

"I'm going to kill her," Matt announced flatly, moving as if to rise.

Brooke stopped him with a hand on his arm, the humor of the situation getting to her. Swallowing a chuckle, she spoke calmly to her infuriated lover. "She was only trying to help."

"It was so stupid for the two of you to be apart," Melinda said with simple logic. "You were both miserable, but neither of you knew how to take the first step to get back together. Pride," she added sternly, "has no place in a relationship, you two."

Brooke laughed quietly, her hand tightening on Matt's arm as he grimly started to climb out of the bed again. "Let me go," he ordered.

Still laughing, she hung on firmly. "No, Matt. You can't kill your sister. I want her to be my maid of honor."

"Have you lost your mind?"

"All right! You're getting married!" Melinda exclaimed over Matt's disbelieving outburst, clasping her hands in delight. "When?"

"At the end of the week. In Springfield," Brooke explained.

"See? I *knew* the two of you belonged together. You only—"

"Let's get something straight right now," Matt broke in, leaning forward as he stared straight into his sister's eyes. "I will not sit here and be lectured on my love life by a smartass teenager. Brooke and I *do* belong together, and we would have straightened everything out without your interference, so your dramatics were totally unnecessary. Now get out of here so Brooke and I can get dressed. And if you have any sense at all," he finished ominously, "you'll be very, very quiet for the rest of the day. Do you understand?"

"Yes, Matt," Melinda answered with proper meekness, though her green eyes, so like his, glinted with mischief. "See you later, Brooke."

"Okay. And Melinda?"

"Yeah?"

Brooke smiled. "Thanks."

Melinda tossed her a thumbs-up sign, meekness disappearing. "Anytime, kid." She was laughing as the bedroom door closed behind her.

"*Must* you encourage her?" Matt demanded, turning to Brooke with a scowl.

Dissolving into giggles, Brooke tried to steady her voice to answer. "I can't help it, Matt. She went to such lengths to get you to fire her and then make me do so. You have to admit she's inventive."

"She's frightening."

Brooke laughed again. "That, too."

"We *would* have gotten back together without her," Matt told her sternly. "I would have come after you soon. I was only giving you time to realize how much you missed me."

"Yes, Matt," Brooke replied, imitating Melinda's assumed meekness.

Matt glared at her for a moment, then shook his head, his lips twitching. "You're both frightening."

"I love you, Matt."

He scooted closer to her, his eyes gleaming with familiar intent.

Brooke backed off. "Now, Matt, we can't do that right now."

"Why not?" he challenged, lifting one hand to wind it in her tangled hair.

"Melinda's in the next room."

"She has enough sense to leave us alone for a while."

"We haven't had breakfast. And since we skipped dinner last night, I'm starving."

"I'll feed you," he promised, his mouth hovering just over hers. "Later."

"I have to work today," she tried again, though her voice was growing weaker.

"You're going to be late." His mouth came down hard on hers, effectively preventing any further argument.

Brooke knew that Matt was deliberately regaining control of the morning that had begun so disconcertingly. He wasn't one to appreciate being manipulated by his younger sister. She really should protest this arrogant compulsion of his to always be in charge, she thought, even as her arms slipped round his neck. And she would have a long talk with him. Later.

Matt pressed her insistently into the pillows, and Brooke arched invitingly beneath him, deciding to soothe the beast before attempting to tame him.

It seemed to be the brightest idea she'd had in years.

COMING IN JUNE

THE MASTER FIDDLER

Jacqui didn't want to go back to college, and she didn't want to go home. Tombstone, Arizona, wasn't in her plans, either, until she found herself stuck there en route to L.A. after ramming her car into rancher Choya Barnett's Jeep. Things got worse when she lost her wallet and couldn't pay for the repairs. The mechanic wasn't interested when she practically propositioned him to get her car back—but Choya was. He took care of her bills and then waited for the debt to be paid with the only thing Jacqui had to offer—her virtue.

Watch for this bestselling Janet Dailey favorite, coming in June from Harlequin.

Also watch for *Something Extra* in August and *Sweet Promise* in October.

JAN-MAS-1

Harlequin Temptation dares to be different!

Once in a while, we Temptation editors spot a romance that's truly innovative. To make sure *you* don't miss any one of these outstanding selections, we'll mark them for you.

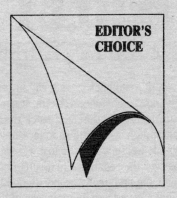

EDITOR'S CHOICE

When the "Editors' Choice" fold-back appears on a Temptation cover, you'll know we've found that extra-special page-turner!

THE *Temptation* EDITORS

You'll flip . . . your pages won't!
Read paperbacks *hands-free* with

Book Mate • I

The perfect "mate" for all your romance paperbacks

Traveling • Vacationing • At Work • In Bed • Studying • Cooking • Eating

Perfect size for all standard paperbacks, this wonderful invention makes reading a pure pleasure! Ingenious design holds paperback books OPEN and FLAT so even wind can't ruffle pages – leaves your hands free to do other things. Reinforced, wipe-clean vinyl-covered holder flexes to let you turn pages without undoing the strap . . . supports paperbacks so well, they have the strength of hardcovers!

Pages turn WITHOUT opening the strap.

SEE-THROUGH STRAP

Reinforced back stays flat.

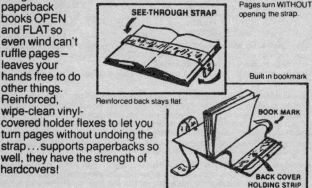

Built in bookmark

BOOK MARK

BACK COVER HOLDING STRIP

10" x 7¼" . opened.
Snaps closed for easy carrying, too

Available now. Send your name, address, and zip code, along with a check or money order for just $5.95 + .75¢ for postage & handling (for a total of $6.70) payable to Reader Service to:

Reader Service
Bookmate Offer
901 Fuhrmann Blvd.
P.O. Box 1396
Buffalo, N.Y. 14269-1396

Offer not available in Canada
*New York and Iowa residents add appropriate sales tax.

BM-G

"GIVE YOUR HEART TO HARLEQUIN" SWEEPSTAKES

OFFICIAL RULES

NO PURCHASE NECESSARY TO ENTER OR RECEIVE A PRIZE

1. To enter and join the Harlequin Reader Service, rub off the concealment device on all game tickets. This will reveal the values for each Sweepstakes entry number and the number of free books you will receive. Accepting the free books will automatically entitle you to also receive a free bonus gift. If you do not wish to take advantage of our introduction to the Harlequin Reader Service but wish to enter the Sweepstakes only, rub off the concealment device on tickets #1-3 only. To enter, return your entire sheet of tickets. Incomplete and/or inaccurate entries are not eligible for that section or sections of prizes. Not responsible for mutilated or unreadable entries or inadvertent printing errors. Mechanically reproduced entries are null and void.

2. Either way, your Sweepstakes numbers will be compared against the list of winning numbers generated at random by computer. In the event that all prizes are not claimed, random drawings will be held from all entries received from all presentations to award all unclaimed prizes. All cash prizes are payable in U.S. funds. This is in addition to any free, surprise or mystery gifts that might be offered. The following prizes are awarded in this sweepstakes:

(1)	*Grand Prize	$1,000,000	Annuity
(1)	First Prize	$35,000	
(1)	Second Prize	$10,000	
(3)	Third Prize	$5,000	
(10)	Fourth Prize	$1,000	
(25)	Fifth Prize	$500	
(5000)	Sixth Prize	$5	

   *The Grand Prize is payable through a $1,000,000 annuity. Winner may elect to receive $25,000 a year for 40 years, totaling up to $1,000,000 without interest, or $350,000 in one cash payment. Winners selected will receive the prizes offered in the Sweepstakes promotion they receive.
   Entrants may cancel the Reader Service at any time without cost or obligation to buy (see details in center insert card).

3. Versions of this Sweepstakes with different graphics may appear in other mailings or at retail outlets by Torstar Corp. and its affiliates. This promotion is being conducted under the supervision of Marden-Kane, Inc., an independent judging organization. By entering the Sweepstakes, each entrant accepts and agrees to be bound by these rules and the decisions of the judges, which shall be final and binding. Odds of winning are dependent upon the total number of entries received. Taxes, if any, are the sole responsibility of the winners. Prizes are nontransferable. All entries must be received by March 31, 1990. The drawing will take place on April 30, 1990, at the offices of Marden-Kane, Inc., Lake Success, N.Y.

4. This offer is open to residents of the U.S., Great Britain and Canada, 18 years or older, except employees of Torstar Corp., its affiliates, and subsidiaries, Marden-Kane, Inc. and all other agencies and persons connected with conducting this Sweepstakes. All federal, state and local laws apply. Void wherever prohibited or restricted by law.

5. Winners will be notified by mail and may be required to execute an affidavit of eligibility and release that must be returned within 14 days after notification. Canadian winners will be required to answer a skill-testing question. Winners consent to the use of their name, photograph and/or likeness for advertising and publicity in conjunction with this and similar promotions without additional compensation. One prize per family or household.

6. For a list of our most current major prizewinners, send a stamped, self-addressed envelope to: WINNERS LIST, c/o MARDEN-KANE, INC., P.O. BOX 701, SAYREVILLE, N.J. 08872

LTY-H49